THE FOXGLOVE TREE

Recent Titles by Elizabeth Gill from Severn House

THE FOXGLOVE TREE
THE HOMECOMING
HOME TO THE HIGH FELLS
THE PREACHER'S SON
WHEN DAY IS DONE
WHERE CURLEWS CRY

THE FOXGLOVE TREE

Elizabeth Gill

This first world edition published in Great Britain 2006 by
SEVERN HOUSE PUBLISHERS LTD of
9–15 High Street, Sutton, Surrey SM1 1DF.
This first world edition published in the USA 2006 by
SEVERN HOUSE PUBLISHERS INC of
595 Madison Avenue, New York, N.Y. 10022.

British Library Cataloguing in Publication Data

Gill, Elizabeth, 1950-
    The foxglove tree
    1. World War, 1914-1918 - Veterans - England - Durham - Fiction
    2. Love stories
    I. Title
    823.9'14 [F]

    ISBN-13: 978-0-7278-6401-7
    ISBN-10: 0-7278-6401-7

All Severn House titles are printed on acid-free paper.

Typeset by Palimpsest Book Production Ltd.,
Polmont, Stirlingshire, Scotland.
Printed and bound in Great Britain by
MPG Books Ltd., Bodmin, Cornwall.

In memory of Bill, who always inspired me

One

Heath Houses Colliery, Durham City, 1917

Erin looked across the small dark front room at her friend. It was almost impossible to know what to say. A telegram was the thing you most dreaded. She and her mam and dad had had such a thing six months before when their John was killed and she didn't think they would ever get over it. Her mam cried all the time and her dad just kept on going to work every day and nobody said anything.

Now Lilian's husband had died and she had had a nice letter from the officer, Major Armstrong, saying how valuable Norman had been, how missed by his friends, how brave. It had been three weeks since and Erin felt she should have known enough to give Lilian some comfort. Only she didn't. She couldn't think what to say that wouldn't sound daft.

It was Saturday. On Saturdays in her house, just two down along the row, her mam would be in the kitchen making egg and chips for tea, which she always did, face red from turning the chips in their frying pan over the fire and the smell was wonderful.

Here was no activity of any kind, no fire, no noise. The door to the kitchen was closed, so presumably Mrs Coulthard, Norman's mam, was next door but you couldn't hear anything.

Lilian had had a baby just three weeks ago so Norman had never seen his little girl. Lilian looked awful. She had the baby in her arms and it had been screaming for the last hour. Finally it quietened.

'His mam says I've got to get out,' Lilian said.

'What does she mean? Where could you go?'

1

'I don't know.'

Mrs Coulthard did not like her daughter-in-law, it was known. She had called her 'that mucky black bitch' to several people, according to Erin's mother. Erin's mam was always saying that Mrs Coulthard was a low, nasty woman and that she couldn't understand how their Norman had turned out such a canny lad but Erin knew that from the minute Norman had taken Lilian home his mam had treated her badly.

Lilian wasn't black but she was coloured, she had brown skin and black hair and black eyes. In some places she might have been thought beautiful but Erin couldn't imagine how her mam would have reacted if their John had come home with a coloured girl and announced he was marrying her.

Worse still that he had to because she was in the family way. Uncharitable people said Lilian had done it on purpose because it was the only road she could follow to get a man but Erin thought she must have been desperate indeed to want to come to such a cheerless place as this tiny pit village on the edge of the city.

'You could come and work at the factory with me and his mam could mind the bairn,' she suggested. Erin made uniforms at the clothing factory down by the river in the town.

'I said that but she wouldn't have it.'

Erin was about to suggest that Lilian and the baby should come and stay with them but she knew it wasn't possible. Her mam wouldn't let anybody into their John's bedroom. She kept the door closed and went in and did not come out for hours at a time. Her bedroom was tiny so Lilian couldn't stop there and her mam and dad slept downstairs. There was no room for anybody.

She wanted to be able to offer Lilian money but she tipped up her wages to her mother and had nothing. Not that her mam kept her short. Considering they were in the middle of a war they did very well. It was just that her mother wouldn't think she needed to have money of her own. She certainly wouldn't be keen on the idea of Erin giving it away. John was dead and Dad was getting old. She would say they had to hang on to every penny.

2

'Do you not have any family?' It was the first time she had said such a thing to Lilian since they had first met down the back lane five months ago when the baby was only just beginning to show. Lilian gave a grim laugh. Her white teeth flashed for a second before she recovered her composure. She shook her head.

'Do you think I would have come here if I'd had somewhere else to go?' she said.

'Where do you come from?'

'North Shields. I lived there with my mam until she died.'

'And your dad?'

'Didn't know him.'

What she meant was that her dad was likely some foreign sailor or the sort and her mam had got mixed up with him and they were probably not married. The story got worse and worse, Erin decided, but that was what people said.

'I wish I could help,' she said.

Lilian looked surprised. And that, Erin thought later, was the worst part of the whole thing.

'Oh, Erin, I didn't expect you to,' she said and she sounded so grateful.

When Erin went down the back lane and up her own yard she explained to her mother what had happened but all her mother said was, 'She should never have got herself into that sort of predicament in the first place,' and sniffed.

Why was it always the woman to blame? Erin wondered. She thought if such a thing had happened to their John her mother would have blamed the girl.

'I'd like to help,' she insisted. 'She has no family, nowhere to go.'

'Erin, you would believe anybody.'

'She hasn't,' Erin said. 'Can I give her some of my wage?'

She spent the entire evening trying to talk her mother into it so it was late and dark when she finally managed to prise a whole pound out of her mother. She ran down the back yard, clashing the gate, stumbled over a big stone and then up the yard of the Coulthard house. She hammered on the back door for a long time in the cold until finally she heard

3

the bolts go back and the key turn. There stood Mrs Coulthard, pale eyes hostile.

'What do you want?' she said.

'I want to see Lilian.'

'Well, you can't. She isn't here any more,' Mrs Coulthard said and closed the door.

Steffie Coulthard heard the girl run down the yard and only then did she let go of her breath. Norman was dead. Norman's dad was dead and the girl was finally gone. She would have the peace, the silence. It was the only thing that was left. She tried to think of good times, of her mother calling her 'Stephanie', of her dad throwing her up to the ceiling and catching her when she came down but it was all too long ago. She could hardly remember the sound of their voices, could not envisage their faces.

She could not bear the shame which her son had brought her. Anybody would have done except that girl. She closed her eyes and listened. The fire crackled and in the back room she thought there was an inch of sherry left over from Christmas. She would have that. It would comfort her.

Two

Allan Jamieson had spent all afternoon in the arboretum at his home, Hedleyhope House, where his godmother's parents and their parents before them had planted hundreds of trees. It wasn't that he wanted to be there, it was just that he didn't want to be anywhere else. The day had not really grown light, the only brightness was the sleet. It was as though it couldn't decide whether to turn to rain or to snow and fell wet and heavy into the thick January earth.

Oak leaves were brown upon the paths, and beechnut kernels. A squirrel ran up a sweet chestnut and there were variegated ivies everywhere. Further over was the monkey puzzle, so tall that you had to stand way back to see the top, and on the ground beneath it the cones lay long and thick like lambs' tails.

He walked past the Himalayan birch trees with their smooth white bark, pieces of black showing through where the outside had been lost. The stone steps were narrow down to the grove where bamboo flourished eight feet high with tiny leaves. The noise of them was like a whisper in the cold wind, their green and white a relief in the gathering dusk, their stems bushy.

On the birch trees parasites called witches' brooms seemed almost menacing with their tiny intricate twigs in a bundle and then as he walked back up towards the house lavender bloomed and rosemary in thick full green, and pansies, yellow, black, purple, violet, white, damson-coloured and pale cream with yellow middles.

He stood back slightly and thought how much he loved Hedleyhope House, which his godmother had left him when she died. It was red-brick, with bay windows on the ground

5

and first floors, and little dormer windows in black and white above on the top storey, with its own woods which went on for several acres to the south side of the small city.

There were conservatories with cacti, tall and thin, and some big with round spiky leaves like frying pans, ponds with goldfish and brightly coloured other fish and more ponds outside and little wooden bridges. Long white grasses with big feathered tops to them swayed in the stiff wind.

The lights were on in the house now and the summer houses in the corners of the garden showed as nothing but shadow as he came back up the hill. Even then he lingered. Only when it was completely dark did he go around to the back of the house, take off his muddy shoes and venture into the main hall.

His wife, Kaye, must have heard him, because she came into the hall. Every time he saw Kaye – and they had been apart so much these past three years – he wondered at her beauty. She was pale, accentuating her startling blue eyes, her skin ivory against her neat black dress.

'Wasn't it awful?' she said. She meant the funeral of her cousin Jake's wife, Madeline.

The funeral had taken most of the day and even though Allan had known lots of soldiers in France who had died you never got used to it, he thought, it never ceased to be shocking and it never should and somehow it was the more shocking that Jake's young wife had died in childbirth while he was not there. When a young woman died like that and her husband was away from home and the baby did not survive . . . What could be worse?

But it was worse somehow because Kaye had never liked Madeline. Kaye, he had thought lately, came from a class of women who wanted everybody to be like she was, she resented Madeline, even though on the surface Madeline was just like everybody else.

She disliked Madeline because she was clever instead of beautiful and yet had managed to marry one of the brightest men in the area. Madeline must therefore, it was reasoned, have employed some wiles which beautiful women did not, something which was not allowed. It upset the order of

6

things. For most women their beauty was all they had. Madeline had somehow broken the rules.

Allan understood Kaye's dilemma. Kaye's parents had died when she was very young and she was always afraid everything would be taken away from her and she believed, though Allan had told her differently hundreds of times, that all she had was her beauty so for other women to win by other ways was somehow a cheat.

Madeline's appeal had nothing whatsoever to do with conventional beauty though to him she had had the most wonderful grey eyes, it was the way that she laughed, the way that she understood immediately what you were saying to her, her enthusiasm for every scheme you had thought up in boyhood and other things, since they had known her all their lives. Madeline was part of it.

Now she was dead, put into the cold earth with her still-born child and Kaye was awkward because you won so completely when the person you had disliked died. For years she and her aunt and their friends had said they had no idea why Jake should have married such a woman. Now he was horribly tragically free and Kaye was feeling guilty as well as sorrowful.

Allan followed his wife into the drawing room and she poured tea. Then she looked at him.

'What are we to do?'

'I thought I would go over later and take him out for a drink.'

'That's a good idea,' Kaye said and then she began to cry, which she hadn't that day.

'Oh, don't,' he said.

'Jake looked like the world was coming to an end.'

Kaye was fond of Jake, rather like Allan had been of Madeline except even more so since he was her cousin. She and her brother, Reginald, had been brought up by Jake's mother and father, their mothers having been sisters.

The family had been so very proud of Jake's exceptional abilities, expected him to marry well, instead of which he had come home with a plain stick of a person who taught primary-school children and came from the kind of back-

7

ground where her father was a clerk in an office and they lived in a very ordinary terraced house.

Worse still Madeline seemed not to notice either that she was socially beneath him or that Jake was considered the cream of the family. She treated him with irreverence, calling him 'idiot face!' when she was angry with him, not knowing or caring that other people were there. She was just as likely to kiss him in public and perhaps it was only in Allan's mind that Madeline had held Jake's head and told him how much she loved him on more than one occasion.

It was one of her most attractive traits, Allan thought, that she cared nothing for money or that Jake was a prosecuting barrister. They had set up home by the river in Durham, in a house which Allan had grown to love, full of books and Madeline's magical presence. She would greet people at the door, make you feel like you were the only person in the world who mattered and pour tea, sit you by the fire, listen entranced to all you had to tell her and be funny.

She made you laugh. He had always been glad to be there, sorry to leave. During the past three years he and Jake had been in France and Madeline's sunny side had suffered from their absence and her worry that Jake should be killed and then she was pregnant and everything was all right, only it wasn't.

Recalled from France, Jake arrived to find his young wife dead. He had not even been able to say goodbye. Allan could not think of anything which would help now.

Jake heard his mother come into the room but he didn't turn back from the big window which looked down the gardens from his parents' house and over to the cathedral. From there it was ten minutes' walk across Framwellgate Bridge, up Silver Street, through the Market Place and up Claypath bank to the house where he had left his wife those few short months ago. It felt like so much further now as though it had almost ceased to exist, the pretty house with the weeping willows when she had been pregnant with their first child and he had had to go away to war and leave her.

'Would you – would you like some tea, darling?'

He was about to refuse but her voice was so tentative, so

8

nervous, almost breaking. It seemed to him that it had been on the point of breaking all day but had not done so. He made himself turn around and smile. His mother was dark and pretty, even through the anxiety.

'That would be lovely,' he said.

She nodded and hurried out. Encouraged, his father, short, bearded, face grey with concern, ventured into the room, walking about by the fireplace. The mourners were gone and the house seemed strangely empty. The noise of their talk, however subdued, had kept the loneliness, the emptiness and the silence at bay. Now it was as though there was nothing between it and him. Jake took to staring down the garden again. He couldn't bear his father's kind blue eyes.

'Do you have to go back tomorrow?'

Jake managed a smile.

'It's a war, you know, Dad. They don't stop it just because I'm not there.'

'Then they should be able to manage without you for a while longer.'

Jake didn't like to say that he wanted to go, that he felt there was nothing left, that in France he might even sometimes be able to pretend to himself that Madeline was still waiting for him in Durham.

'Is there anything you would like me to do?' his father asked.

Jake shook his head.

'I haven't said much to you, Jake, but I am so very sorry. Madeline was a wonderful girl and we are devastated because of the loss of our grandchild. We will do everything we can to help you.'

It was not true, of course, they had never liked her, but it was safe to speak well of her because she was dead. Jake turned around.

'Thank you. You always do,' he said. He would be glad to back to war. There was nothing left here but his parents, so sad for him and they had each other. His mother came back with a tray, carrying it herself. They had help but he thought she did not want anybody intruding upon their grief, as though Milly or Mrs Gainsborough would have been intrusive.

They had both been there for years. Most of the other servants had got caught up in the war, as they had no doubt thought they should, as he had thought he should, the women into the munitions factories, the men in France, but the servants left in his parents' house were too old for any of these things.

His mother set down the silver tray upon the low table by the fire and offered cake which he refused. He would have choked.

Then she said to him, 'You must come back and live at home.'

'I can't do that.'

'Where else would you go?'

'You've had enough to cope with already.'

'Stay with us,' she urged him, 'at least until the war is over.'

Jake was beginning to think it would never be over but he didn't say this.

After tea what he really wanted to do was to go out and get very, very drunk but he couldn't because he knew they would worry. He could not help being grateful when in the early evening Allan arrived and offered to go for a drink with him.

The weather had got worse. Jake was only glad for the inside of the pub. Here he could pretend that he was going back home to Madeline, that his last sight had not been her waving him away on the train four months earlier, that he would see her again, take her into his arms, feel her, speak to her.

'How was Kaye?' he asked.

Allan and Kaye had managed a row before he left. Funny how funerals made you turn on one another. People got drunk and shouted. People stayed sober and shouted. It was nothing to do with the funeral, of course, it was to do with Laurie going away to school.

'We put his name down when he was a few months old,' Kaye said, clearly not understanding at all.

'Things were different then,' Allan said and wanted to groan. Why did he have to explain this? Why didn't Kaye know?

'You went there and so did Jake and so did your father and . . .' Allan didn't say anything. 'You agreed to this, Allan.'

Allan looked at her. She was glaring at him.

'Everything's changed. I've been away for almost four years,' he said. 'Laurie is seven. I've hardly seen him since he was three—'

'It's not a matter of mathematics,' Kaye said, so intelligent and cool that Allan wanted to hit her. He realized also and with a surprise that he was used to being obeyed. In France he was Lieutenant Colonel Jamieson and everybody did what he said. 'There's no reason why Laurie should forfeit his education because there is a war.'

'Only his father,' Allan said and then was ashamed of himself.

'You had a choice,' Kaye said.

'I have a choice about where he goes to school.'

'No, you don't. He's too old to get into anywhere else now.'

'What's wrong with the school here?'

'It's here, that's what's wrong with it.'

'What if he wants to stay here?'

The triumph in Kaye's eyes was barely hidden and Allan could not remember why he had agreed to any of this.

'Shall we call him in and ask him?' she said and had had the child called into the drawing room before Allan could decide which was better.

Laurie looked exactly like his mother, Allan thought as the boy came in, small, slight, fair. He looked like Jake had looked at seven, when they had both been sent away together, they had been friends as children, their parents had been friends, both their fathers were solicitors. The families were still very close. Ought he to tell Kaye that Jake had been so very pretty, just like Laurie and that the older boys had fought to bed him?

Michaels, who had won, had had his head blown off in

11

France. Allan had not forgotten the look of glee in Jake's eyes. Were things any more civilized now? Kaye obviously thought so and it was hardly something they could discuss. Allan wished he could grab Laurie's hand and run down the garden with him, Alice in Wonderland like, to disappear and never come back.

Laurie went straight to his mother. He and Allan were almost strangers.

'We're talking about school,' Kaye said to him, 'Daddy doesn't think you should go.'

Laurie looked blankly at Allan.

'But I want to,' he said.

'Wouldn't you like to stay here in Durham where you could come home every night?' Allan said.

'I'd be a day boy. All my friends are going away to school. You went and so did Grandpa.'

Allan had forgotten the way that the boarders looked down on the day boys, and called them 'peasants'. It was something to do with the way that the day boys got to go home, a kind of horrid envy and a knowledge that you had to be so much harder to endure boarding school, pretending to them that they were missing out on jolly times.

Some of them were of course but he had not forgotten listening to children crying themselves to sleep night after night, neither had he forgotten the longing for his mother, the homesickness which went on and on, the cold classrooms, the stinking lavatories, the grey dormitories, the perpetual beatings, the big boys who were prefects who despised you, the masters you scarcely dared address, the freezing baths, the way that if you did not learn to stand up for yourself, learn to fight, you were ground down.

It had been a good preparation for war. It was nothing to do with real education, he thought, not with any kind of system which tried to make men into decent human beings. No wonder he had been so good at killing other men.

Helplessness, anger, frustration, of being in the sixth form where you had the power to inflict misery if you were weak, either that or be popular amongst the younger boys and lose the respect of your peers, all those feelings left over from

12

school came together in the trenches. Was that what his son could expect?

He thought he had been better equipped for school, if you could be, than this child in front of him. Laurie had suffered from the lack of a father and so had he. Allan's father had died when he was a very small child, he barely remembered him so to an extent he understood, so much so that he did not want Laurie to suffer something which was almost the same.

Laurie was almost completely Kaye's child, Allan thought, with a pain which was physical. He spent hours reading by the library fire, his friends carefully chosen by Kaye. Not for him the rough and tumble of the streets, the small adventures which mattered so much when you were a boy. He had never spent a night away from home, camped on somebody's lawn and been afraid in the dark, dived off a high bridge into deep water or fought another boy for possession of something which seemed so important at the time.

'I want to be like my friends,' Laurie said. Of course he did. Who would wish to be different?

Allan was inclined to make terms, to say that Laurie could leave the minute he disliked it, that they would plan a better life somewhere else, but all he could see in his mind were the eighteen- and nineteen-year-old boys going over the top to screaming injury and death.

'Then you must,' he said.

Allan had been torn between not wanting to leave Jake when it grew late and wanting to go home to Kaye. He tried to do both by staying with Jake until Jake suggested he should go and then hurrying away.

Kaye had already gone to bed. He listened to the silence of the house. When he stood still he imagined he could hear the sound of the bamboo canes in the wind in the garden. Many times when he had been in France and had felt that he could not stand any more he had thought of the gardens here, the peace, the way that the seasons changed the same each year.

He opened the door of his wife's bedroom. She was sitting at the dressing table, brushing her hair. He could remember when her hair had been so long that she could sit on its shining length. Now it was chopped short. She suited it like that, she had the cheekbones for it, but he regretted the change or was it just that it was more than her hairstyle she had altered? She turned.

'How is Jake?'

Allan had to be careful. Jake was her beloved cousin.

'Rather drunk, I think.'

She asked nothing more and Allan felt awkward. Since he had got here she had not asked him into her bedroom. She had gone to bed before him each night and the twice he had tried her door it was locked.

Their earlier quarrel had nothing to do with the way that she looked at him. Allan hovered, waiting to be invited in, hoping she might say something encouraging but she didn't. Finally, instead of going out and closing the door, as he felt he should have done, he came inside.

'Kaye . . .' He wanted to say, 'I'm going back in the morning,' but she knew that so where was the purpose in it? He wanted to say something about being caught up in Madeline's death and funeral and Jake's grief but that seemed pointless too. He wished he could make it across the sea of floor to her but somehow he couldn't. They had barely touched in the few days that he had been at home. 'Kaye . . .' was all he could manage.

She was so beautiful and he wanted her so much and she had obviously not thought that he would come into her room because she wore a cream silk robe over a cream silk nightdress and every curve of her body could be seen.

'No.' It was such a decisive no, short and sharp.

She looked him straight in the eyes.

'No, what?' Allan said, bewildered.

'I can't do this.'

'Do what?'

Kaye got up.

'Must you be so obtuse?' She approached him as though the silver-backed hairbrush was a weapon in her hand. 'I

14

hate it when you leave. I hate that you thought you had to go in the first place—'

'I didn't have any choice!'

'Reggie didn't go.' Reggie, Kaye's brother, had avoided going. 'You were ill. You had rheumatic fever as a small child. You have a damaged heart. You didn't have to, they wouldn't have made you.' The tears were running down Kaye's face. 'Lots of men with less excuse stayed at home. I needed you to stay here, you knew I did.'

Allan hesitated.

'I couldn't do that.'

'You lied. You lied to everybody. My uncle and aunt didn't want you to go and I'm left here bringing up Laurie by myself—'

'Millions of women are the same.'

'But we didn't have to. You didn't think about me. You didn't think how I would be left here worrying in case you died.'

'Hundreds of thousands of men have died. More.'

'I didn't love hundreds of thousands of men. I know it's selfish, I know it is.' The silver-backed hairbrush flashed in the light as she waved her hands in despair. 'But I don't know how to do this on my own. I've lost both my parents and now . . . I don't think I love you any more, Allan, I really don't.' Her voice broke there.

He tried to go towards her but she backed away. 'Don't come any nearer. It's better this way. Go and sleep next door. Please.'

Allan went.

Three

L ilian stood by Elvet Bridge, looking down into the water. She had run out of ideas. She had run out of hope. She had no money. She had nowhere to go. The night was coming down fast and cold. The baby was beginning to cry again. She had barely stopped since Lilian had left Mrs Coulthard's house for the last time, insults ringing in her ears.

She had always known that Norman's mother disliked her and the feelings had grown worse in the short time since he had died. It had occurred to her that his mother might endure her presence there for the sake of her grandchild. It had proved a false hope. Perhaps, she concluded, it would have been different had the child been a boy. Maybe not. Maybe his mother's grief was so bad that she did not consider anyone else at all.

The light had gone. There was nothing but a moon and it had a huge ring around it, a sure sign of frost. The cold was beginning to make its way through her thin clothes. She looked down into the water. There was nothing left. She did not have to endure the night. No one was about. All she had to do was climb up onto the stone of the bridge and jump. It was not very high. She and the baby would be with Norman and everything would be all right.

She chided herself for trying to take the easy way out. How much harder to stay here but without shelter with such a small child, what could she do? There was nothing left.

Lilian had no idea how long she stood there, when a voice beside her said her name and made her jump. How he knew who she was in the moonlight she had no idea.

'Mrs Coulthard?' He sounded surprised.

Lilian turned around. It was Norman's commanding officer,

16

Major Armstrong, whose wife had just died. His family was well known in the town. His dad was a solicitor. He had written her such a nice letter about Norman. She had it in her pocket now.

'What are you doing?' he said.

'Just . . .'

'Isn't it awfully cold and dark to be out here with a baby?'

Lilian wanted to tell him that she had nowhere to go but somehow it seemed such an imposition. Hadn't he just buried his wife? The baby was crying even harder now.

'Come on.' He took her arm and walked her off the bridge and Lilian had not the strength to object.

They went up the steep way that was the beginning of Saddler Street, through the marketplace and up the next steep road which was Claypath and then he turned off along another short cobbled road and in at gates and down the bank and there stood the loveliest house that Lilian had ever seen, bathed in moonlight, solid, square, substantial.

He led her through the yard and in by the back entrance and then disappeared into the depths of the house for a few moments. A light flared. He guided her through into the hall and then into a small well-furnished room. He got down and lit the fire and urged her to sit in what had to be the most comfortable armchair she could ever remember.

She sat there, cradling the baby, watching the flames begin to make their way around the newspaper, sticks and coal.

'I thought it might be damp,' he declared, staying where he was, she thought in fear that it might go out, 'but my mother's been attending to things lately and she's a stickler for getting things right.'

He went away again for a few minutes, disappearing into the relative darkness of the hall while Lilian glanced out of the window. When he had gone she went over. It was a long Georgian window and it looked out at the river and the trees and the little city and it was so beautiful, the gardens in front fell all the way down to where the moon turned the Wear to a silver ribbon.

He came back with a glass and handed it to her.

'Brandy.'

17

'Could I . . . would you mind if I changed the baby?'

'Of course not.'

'On the rug?'

'Certainly. Help yourself.'

She did, taking a rag from the bundle while he tactfully busied himself elsewhere and then she fed the baby and finally, when the baby was wrapped in the thick blanket which was the only thing she had brought which had been Norman's mother's, she put the sleeping child down by the fire, her arms ached so much, she had not let go of the baby for hours. And then there was the satisfaction of watching her child sleep.

'There'll be tea soon. I lit the kitchen stove and I can find you something to eat. Tell me what happened.'

Lilian shook her head.

'Drink your brandy and tell me.'

So she sat down and sipped at the brandy.

'Mrs Coulthard didn't want me there any more.'

'Why ever not?'

He sounded so horrified, so surprised that she looked properly at him for the first time and she liked his bewilderment at her situation. Also he was very nice looking, she thought, with fair hair and brown eyes.

'We married because I was expecting,' Lilian was so ashamed to say it, it made her sound like a loose woman and she wasn't.

She was suddenly desperate to tell this man that Norman had been the first and only and she had not known anything and by the time she realized what was going on it was too late. It had only been once. She couldn't tell him, she could only go on looking into his beautiful eyes.

'It seemed the right thing to do. My mother was never married and . . . I hardly saw him. He was in France and I was left with his mother. After he died she didn't want us because of the baby but today . . .' She took a breath before she said, 'Today I had to leave.'

Major Armstrong sat there, staring into the fire for several moments before he said, 'Have some more brandy,' and he got up and went back to the kitchen and came back and gave her tea with brandy in it since she wouldn't take the brandy

18

on its own. And from somewhere he had managed a cake, a thick rich fruit cake. Lilian was almost happy. She ate two huge pieces. It had been a long time since she had felt so warm and comfortable and then she remembered. It wasn't right for her to put on him. Yet where would she go?

'You can stay here, don't worry,' he said.

Lilian's cheeks went warm, in spite of her situation.

'I can't do that, Mr Armstrong.'

'I can stay with my parents,' he said. 'I'm going back in the morning.'

'I can't put you out of your home.'

'You're not. They'll worry if I don't go there. They're expecting me. I've lit the fire upstairs and the bed's made up. Let me show you.'

'I can't,' Lilian said.

He looked at her and it was the first time Lilian thought how lovely he was and it wasn't just his looks, he was kind.

'You think I would let this house stand empty when you and your child have nowhere to go?'

Nobody had been this good to her before. Was he the sort of man who expected payment in bed before he left?

'You can stay here as long as you like. I'll get my dad to come and see you and he'll help you.'

He gave her a roll of notes from his pocket. She protested but when she wouldn't take them he put them on the dresser.

'You can get a job later and pay me back,' he said.

He showed her into a pretty bedroom at the back of the house which looked out over the drive and the trees and by then she was too tired and too grateful to argue with him. As they went back downstairs, just before he left she managed, 'I'm so sorry about your wife.'

'Thank you. Try not to worry about things. Just think about the baby.'

She barely had time to tell him how she felt before he was gone and then she went back upstairs and got into bed, and held the baby close and was only awake long enough to marvel at how her luck had changed before everything blurred and she slept.

*   *   *

19

Jake expected his parents would be in bed, instead of which they were waiting by the fire and he was obliged to tell them what he had done. They were too sensitive as to what had happened that day to oppose him but he knew that they were not pleased or happy about the arrangement. He didn't care. He told them without further explanation and then he went to bed, only pausing on the stairs as his father followed him out of the room to say, 'Promise me you'll find her some kind of job. She needs the money.'

'Don't worry,' his father said.

Jake didn't sleep. He was too aware of being here for the first time without Madeline now that she was buried. He felt even stranger than he had felt on the previous nights, lying in his parents' house again as though he were a child and of course he was going back to the Front in the morning but Allan would be with him.

The thing which comforted Jake most that night was of thinking about Lilian Coulthard and her baby sleeping safely in his house. He could almost believe that Madeline and his child were still there.

Four

Erin considered whether to go and see Kelvin McCormack, John's best friend. He was home for a few days, so she had heard. Erin had got used to the idea of their John not coming back. At least she thought she had. When Kelvin came home by himself which he did that January he had not been home for two years.

She walked down the back street of the pit row and put her head around the door of the house which had been theirs and said to the woman in the doorway, 'Is Kelvin in, Mrs Trevors?'

'No, he isn't. This isn't his house any more. I told him.'

'I think he knows that,' Erin said.

'Well then,' Mrs Trevors said and closed the door.

It was true that the Trevors family, being miners, were now entitled to the house and that Kelvin, being away in France fighting, for some unjust reason was not. His father had died while he was away and he had been the miner in the family. The rule was one man one house, perhaps especially now when things were so difficult. But, Erin thought, at the rate men were being killed you would think the housing situation would ease and then she realized what she had thought and winced.

She chided herself for being so mean and hung about in the back lane, wondering whether Kelvin had gone to the pub. He had not been to their house, though her mother said he had been sighted yesterday, but her dad had not been able to unearth him, even though he had gone round the pubs.

She was just about to give up when she saw his slight figure turn the corner into their road and there was something reluctant about the way that he walked, as there would be.

'Kelvin,' she cried and had to not cast herself at him.

21

Such gestures were unacceptable, even after so long. He looked exhausted, pale, almost grey, his eyes had lost most of their colour and all of their light somehow and his eyes had been his best feature, green and mischievous.

'How are you?' she said.

'I'm grand.'

'I went to your house—'

'It isn't our house any more,' he said, with understandable bitterness.

'Come to mine. My mam and dad will be glad to see you and you can stay for tea,' she said, putting her hand through his arm and though he protested she dragged him up the back lane and in at her yard gate.

She knew why he was reluctant, he had not been in there since John had been killed and John was the only son in the family and he would know how her mother and father felt, how unfair it was that John should die. Her mam, however, would not hold that against a lad she had always liked.

'Why, Kelvin, wherever have you been? I thought you'd come straight here. You want nothing with that mucky woman who's got your house.'

'Mam,' Erin protested, but her mother brushed her aside, sat Kelvin down by the kitchen fire and gave him tea. It was almost, Erin thought, as though their John had come home.

She was surprised that Kelvin's presence gave her mam comfort though the two lads had always been good friends so it shouldn't have been. To Erin, Kelvin looked all wrong without their John but it did not seem so to her mother, she could tell or maybe her mother was by now used to making the best of everything that happened.

'You must come and stay here. Mrs Trevors isn't a nice woman and she's nothing to do with you.'

'There's nothing much left. Not even a stick of furniture,' Kelvin said. 'I wonder what they did with it?'

'We cleared your things out. The decent furniture is either next door or upstairs in my back room and your dad's clothes and his books and all your stuff is here. Don't you be worrying about it,' she said and Erin thought that both she and Kelvin looked better for the meeting.

Her mother gave Kelvin John's room, where his furniture was, much to Erin's astonishment but where else would he sleep and why should she not? Erin had been conscious that when John was alive – and it seemed awful to say it – she was always second best.

Since then she had been moved into first, no, only place. Now, that evening, it was as though she was lagging behind in the affection stakes once more as her mother cosseted Kelvin. She told herself that it was just because he was going back to war but it was not.

A light had come on in her parents' eyes. When her father came home he greeted Kelvin like the son he was not and Erin felt worse because Kelvin had lost his home and his only parent. Why did she feel so badly?

It was revealed to her the next morning when Kelvin tried to kiss her by following her into the front room. She was jealous of how much Kelvin seemed to care for her parents and not the other way round and she wanted him to notice her.

'What are you doing?' she said, pleased and trying not to smile.

'I've missed you so much. Have you got somebody else?'

'No, I haven't,' Erin said. Who would she have? Everybody was away.

She let him kiss her. It was a pleasant sensation there in the quiet of the room which looked out across the street. When he did it again she liked it even more and got her arms up around his neck before the clatter of pots in the kitchen reminded her that her mam was around and she drew back, looking at him as she had never looked at a lad before.

'Will you write to me, Erin?' he said.

'If you like.'

'It would mean a lot to me, to think about you here.'

'No lad's ever asked me to write to him.'

He didn't look at her. Erin thought about all the lads being killed and she couldn't bear to think of it happening to him. He had gone through enough.

'It cannot go on much longer,' she said.

'Will you wait for me?' He looked her directly in the eyes. 'Will you?'

23

'I'm not going anywhere.'

'I didn't mean that.'

'I know what you meant and I will.'

'When I come back . . .' What a brave thing it was to say, she thought, 'We could get wed. Would you, Erin?'

She didn't know what to say and was inclined, like lasses in the daft books she read, to tell him that it was all very sudden and she couldn't decide.

'You're so bonny,' he said.

Nobody had ever paid attention to her like this. Her mam and dad would be pleased.

'Will you, Erin?'

'Aye, I will,' she said and she hugged him.

They didn't tell anybody. She hadn't had a secret before and it was sweet. The following day when the house was empty they sat on the settee in the front room and kissed until Erin was thinking that if she wasn't careful she would end up like Lilian. She stopped his hands from straying below her waist for the third time and sat up.

Luckily at that point the back door slammed so she didn't have to explain herself. God knew what had happened to Lilian. There was no way she could let the world do such things to her. She was going to be in charge of her fate as much as she could. Her mam came in.

'How about making the tea, our Erin?' she said and she smiled at Kelvin.

Her mam would be pleased when they were married, Erin thought.

'What's afoot?' her mam said and he, looking animated for the first time since he had come home said,

'We're going to get wed when I come back—' and then he remembered his manners and said, 'That's if you and Mr Marsden don't mind?'

Her mother's face lit. It was like she had been given an unexpected birthday present.

'Why, that'll be lovely,' she said and immediately began to make plans, how they could live in with them until Kelvin got his job back at the pit and how nice everything would be and she knew that her mam was thinking about grand-

24

bairns and how the first would be a boy and they would be able to call him John. Her mam always made plans so far ahead that it scared Erin.

Her dad came home and he was pleased too and took Kelvin off to the pub to celebrate. Erin wished there was some way women could celebrate. She looked out over the little street and suddenly she thought she could see the future and she wondered if she would be there forever. It was beginning to look rather like a prison. She shrugged off the mood.

He would live through this war and he would come back and everything would be all right and he would get a good job and she would have pretty clothes and a pearl ring and lots of books. She had books but her mother wouldn't have them in the sitting room, they were in her bedroom and her mam complained about the amount of space they took up in such a small house.

Her mother was afraid of books like she was afraid of life beyond this tiny pit community on the edge of Durham. Erin was afraid too but sometimes she was more afraid that this would be all she would ever have. Kelvin would take care of that. He was a clever lad and when he came back they would go and live somewhere else, somewhere pretty, and they would be married and she would have a son and a daughter and her parents could come and visit. She would not be left here in Heath Houses, she would be free.

It was almost two weeks later that she was walking away from the bookshop in Saddler Street. This was the road above Elvet Bridge which wound its cobbled narrow way up towards the cathedral, finally ending in a dramatic sweep before it became Palace Green, and beyond it was the cathedral.

The pavement there was very narrow and could not accommodate all the people who were on it and were not inclined to step into the road so she had to keep moving on and off the cobbles. It was wet, slippery, it had done nothing but rain that week, sleet which melted as it reached the road.

A very smart car stood, a chauffeur about to assist a tall man into it and then somebody behind Erin jostled her and within seconds she had collided with the tall man. Somehow she lost her balance, dropped the parcel of books she had been carrying – they had been bought with her birthday money – and they fell into a large puddle in the gutter, her umbrella shot into the chauffeur's face and if the tall man had not caught her as she knocked against him she would have gone the same way as the books.

'Oh, I'm so sorry,' she said and then she was looking at him.

He had dark eyes, even darker than her own, almost black, which held her gaze in a strange way. He was older than she was, perhaps forty. He held her until she steadied and then he smiled, not quite at her but in her direction generally.

'Your parcel, miss,' the chauffeur said, picking it out of the puddle. 'It's very wet.'

'My apologies,' the tall man said and she liked his voice. She could have gone on listening to him for hours. 'What is your parcel?'

'Books,' Erin said regretfully.

'Can anything be done, Andrews?'

The chauffeur examined the parcel with care. Erin was surprised. Were rich people so stupid that they couldn't even look at a parcel themselves? And then, glancing at him again, she realized that he couldn't see. He gazed beyond them both.

'Don't think so, Sir Angus.'

And then Erin knew who he was. Angus Ballantine. He was some kind of rich lord and lived in a great big house down by the river. He had been hurt in the war and come home.

'It doesn't matter,' she said hastily.

'Oh, but it does,' Sir Angus said. 'The bookshop is just a little way. Let us go back inside and see whether they have other copies.'

The chauffeur would have taken his arm but he caught his fingers on to hers and said, 'Lead the way,' and she did not like to tell him that the books had been second-hand and she did not think they had other copies of them.

Saddler Street was never the same to Erin after that. They went back into the dark depths of the shop and he bought

26

other books for her. He offered her a lift home. The car was a magic ride like carpets in stories, she had never been in one before and her mother would be cross that she had gone in one now with a strange man but he was a war hero and he was quite old. They sat in the back and he told her his name and then he told her that she was beautiful.

'Can you see me?' she couldn't help but ask.

'Not well. I can make out shapes and such. My leg bothers me more.' He had been careful of it when getting into the car.

She told him who she was and where she lived and too short a time later they arrived outside her house. She thanked him. The chauffeur helped her out and she watched as the car drove away and she could not help hoping that her neighbours had noticed.

It was like a fairy tale which she breathlessly related to her mother who had missed the whole thing being busy making tea at the time but when the excitement had gone somehow the joy had gone too and her life had never seemed as dreary. Other people lived in different ways. She could not be satisfied with anything after that. It was as though she was Sleeping Beauty and the bad fairy had waved a wand and she had awoken as somebody new, filled with selfish thoughts.

She could not stop thinking about him, his beautiful voice and his good manners, and her mood was as grey as the rain which never stopped falling until the whole of the little city was shrouded in it.

Her mother came to her one afternoon the following week. Erin had just come back from the factory.

'That man sent you a note yesterday. I nearly put it on the fire but I couldn't bring myself,' her mother said.

'What man?'

'The one who gave you a lift in his car.'

'Have you got it?'

Her mother reached into her skirt pocket and took out a long white envelope.

'It's been opened,' Erin objected.

'Aye, I know it has. I haven't shown your father.'

27

Erin read. It was to invite her to tea at Broke Hall. She read it twice and then looked at her mother's grim expression.

'Men like that only have one thing in mind with girls like you and it's not tea,' she said.

'It sounds all right.'

'I know what it sounds like. You have Kelvin. You want nowt with folk like them. I shouldn't say this to you, Erin, but your trouble is that you're far too bonny for your own good. I don't know where you got it from but it's something that the good Lord didn't mean for women to make use of in that way. You go up there and then he'll start offering you money, buying you things and before you know it he'll be wanting things in return. And we know what that means, don't we?'

'I want to go,' she said. 'It's next Sunday.'

Her mother shook her head.

This was nothing to do with how she felt about Kelvin. Angus Ballantine was old, she could not think of him the same way.

Sir Angus had said that he would send the chauffeur for Erin but since she wanted nobody to know what she was doing she was down past the end of the road long before the time the car would arrive. Even so people stared and she thought it would not be long before everybody knew what she had done. It was difficult, her mother would not help but neither had she given Erin away to her father so all she could do was to wear her best frock, which was nothing special, and hope that she was not making some awful kind of mistake.

She had stupid visions of Angus Ballantine locking her into a tower but these all went when she saw his house.

The road went through the centre of Durham and then turned off, once the car had crossed the river, on to a small road and then through large black iron gates. Erin had heard stories about people falling in love. She had not known that people fell in love with houses. She could not imagine feeling half as much for any man as she felt for Broke Hall when she went there for the first time.

It was nothing like she had thought it would be. She had known it would not be a castle, people like Sir Angus would live in fairly ordinary houses. After all he was not a duke or an earl or something like that.

The road which led up to the house was steep and winding, through the meadow and then past various tiny intricate hidden gardens to the side but not before Erin had a glimpse of the front. It was Georgian, three-storeyed and narrow with a long cottage garden and to one side what seemed to her like an earlier part in brick and at the other end another entirely different bit as though succeeding generations had had a bit of money and added on more comfort or something ambitious. The chauffeur stopped, opened the door for her and a small red-faced middle-aged woman came out of the back door, smiling and saying, 'Do come in. I'm Angus's sister, Diana.' It seemed incongruous somehow that he should have a sister as old as her parents. The little woman was slight-boned, dressed in grey with grey hair and not the fashion-conscious figure which Erin always supposed rich people were. They went into the kitchen.

'I'm afraid we shall have to shift for ourselves. We can't get staff, what with the war and everything. I have made scones.'

They were very nice scones, Erin thought, as later they sat around the fire of a large and draughty drawing room which had a log fire burning in a huge open grate, a wonderful view of the town and the cathedral and more overgrown gardens.

Sir Angus was not quite so glamorous either, sitting about his fire wearing a thick cardigan against the cold and looking every year of however old he was but then soldiers did look old. Kelvin looked more like thirty than twenty and Sir Angus had been badly hurt.

When they went into the kitchen Diana said, 'You mustn't mind him. It's all been too much. His fiancée jilted him, you know, when she discovered he had lost his sight. It was kind of you to come.'

As though she was doing them a favour, Erin thought in amazement. How silly her mother had been to think that these people were some kind of threat. Later, just before it got dark, she and Angus walked around the gardens and they were so pretty, one leading into another through wrought-iron gates, a big pond at the back of the property and high walls so that you couldn't quite see into the next garden, through a gate either wooden or iron.

There were hidden seats and climbing roses and even though it was winter pink flowers – she did not know their name, some kind of shrub – blossomed close to the black soil.

Angus kissed her hand and told her how good it was of her to come and see them and brighten their dull lives. She must come again some time. He was not specific and neither was his sister when Erin left and she could hardly ask them back to Lilac Street at the far side of the town where the pit-owner's wife, back in the old days, had been a gardener and named the pit terraces Heather, Camellia and Lilac.

Her dad and the other men thought it was funny and said things could have been worse, they could have been living in Rhododendron Row or Buttercup Avenue, but Erin always went warm at the idea of Lilac Street. It was awful. The little back-to-back terraces where a lilac tree had never yet been seen, nothing to them but yards with lavatories and coal houses.

Erin was home before her dad came in for his tea and it had never looked so dark, so shabby, no outlook, nowhere to breathe, nothing to see. She explained to her mother how kind they had been, both Angus and his sister, and how pretty their house was. All her mother said was, 'Make that do, then,' and she got on with preparing the meal for her husband coming home.

30

Five

Diana watched her brother make his way carefully around the garden beyond the drawing room. He walked with a stick, putting it before him in case there should be any obstacle. She had tried to make sure that there was nothing in his way, she had dragged anything which he might encounter into the corners of the garden, such as it was these days.

She could remember when it had been well tended, well kept, when they had two gardeners. Now the only help they had was the chauffeur, who came in for two hours a week which was all they could afford, when they journeyed into Newcastle or Durham. They didn't go further than that, there wasn't any point, they had very little money and no motive. It looked good, she had to acknowledge, but the truth was that they had nothing. Angus was even considering getting rid of the car. What did it matter about going places, he said, when he couldn't see them. The garden was far enough for him, he could find his way around it.

When she had been much younger and prettier she had managed to attract the attention of a man with money but he had left her for somebody beautiful and since that time she had lived at home, growing older and plainer, and she had lost hope of ever marrying suitably or at all for that matter.

Lately she had looked on younger men and wondered what it was like to be held in someone's arms. All she had were the memories of being eighteen, the dancing, the headiness of thinking someone might be in love with her.

It didn't seem to matter. Angus had been engaged to a rich girl. Everything would be all right. He had status and the house, charm, intelligence, background and looks. She had money and even though Diana hadn't particularly liked her she knew how much they needed the input of cash. It was as simple as that.

Now her brother was as unlikely to marry well as she was. Who would put up with him, disabled, blind and poor? She watched as he came back in from the garden, she heard him shuffle along the hall.

'Di?' Like a lost child.

'I'm here.'

She waited until he came into the room. She made herself not help him, he hated it, and when he was sitting by the fire she went across and sat in the chair opposite.

'Do you think Miss Marsden would come back?'

'I'm sure she would if you asked.'

'Did you like her?'

'She seems a very pleasant sort of girl and we have so little company these days.'

'I think we shall have to sell this place soon.'

Strange how his mind ran on.

'Who would want to buy it? It's dropping apart. I've sold every decent piece of jewellery I possess, all the good furniture and the ornaments and paintings are gone. We barely have enough to live on.'

He laughed and there was a harsh resigned note to it.

'You mean one of us needs to marry money.'

'Yes, indeed, though to be realistic I hardly think it's likely any more.'

'She is a nice girl, though,' he said, 'she smells of the country, like lavender after rain. She liked the house.'

'You'd like the house if you came from a pit cottage. They live in hovels somewhere out towards Bowburn, don't they?'

'Heath Houses.'

It was, she thought, a tiny pit village on the outskirts of the city with one street, a few pubs and a pit.

'I would like to see her again. I know,' he went on, even though Diana hadn't said anything, 'that she's not suitable but I feel as though I would like to marry someone. Don't you feel like that?'

'Very much but there isn't a lot of choice. Even young

and beautiful women have difficulty in finding someone. How would I?'

'If they knew how nice you were they would flock here.'

She kissed him on the forehead and said that she would see about dinner.

'And I shall go down to the cellar and find a decent bottle of wine. There have to be some compensations.'

Later, when they had drunk their wine, slowly, and eaten their dinner even more slowly since he was clumsy, there was nothing left but the firelight. She was about to offer to read to him when he said, 'Would you ask her to come here again?'

Diana promised that she would write and ask Miss Marsden to come back the very next Saturday and he said that would be lovely and would give him something to look forward to.

If he wanted to see a common girl with a thick accent then it was up to him. The girl was ignorant, uneducated and totally without charm as far as Diana could see but Angus did not have much choice and presumably he was as keen to bed a beautiful young body as any other man. It seemed to be all men cared for.

If he should decide he wanted to marry Erin Marsden then she would have to put up with it and it would destroy the one thing she had left, the uninterrupted peace. She would have to put up with another woman in the house.

But then maybe Erin was good in the house, if she could cook and bake and would help with the cleaning and the garden then it might be a good thing having her around and maybe they would even have a child and that made her feel very excited.

She would have a nephew or a niece, a child not quite hers but close enough. She would be Aunt Di. How nice that would be. Perhaps she would be right to encourage Erin Marsden. Angus could not look any higher than a pitman's daughter, it seemed, but they might have some joy from it yet.

She sat up in bed the next morning and imagined the note she would send, how much they had enjoyed Miss Marsden's company and would she care to come for supper on Saturday.

33

It seemed unlikely that Erin would refuse. She seemed to have nothing in her life but her parents, she had not mentioned a young man, only her brother who had died on the Somme.

The note was answered within a day. Miss Marsden would be delighted to come to supper. Angus smiled all day after she read it out to him.

'If you're going to go there again you'll have to tell your father,' her mother said. She didn't look at Erin when she said it.

'What does it matter?'

'You know it does.'

Erin didn't want to do that. Her father didn't like what he called toffee-nosed folk but she knew that if she didn't tell him her mother would, so on the Friday night just as he was about to go off to the pub, dressed in his best suit, she said, 'I've been invited to tea with some people tomorrow.'

'Have you? That's nice, love.'

'They live in a big house by the river, Broke Hall.'

'Oh aye?' He was looking at himself in the mirror above the mantelpiece in the kitchen. He wasn't listening, she could tell, he was no doubt thinking about being in the pub with his friends, drinking and talking and smoking and enjoying himself. It was all right for men to enjoy themselves.

'You don't mind, then?'

'Eh?' She had caught his attention but he wasn't really listening as she had known he would not be. Erin just smiled. He turned to the doorway. 'I'm off to the pub, Sadie.'

'Now there's a surprise,' his wife said as she came through from the front room. She had been doing it out for Sunday. They always sat in there on Sunday afternoons. Erin was learning to hate the monotony of their life.

'It's only once a week, lass.'

'Get yourself away, then, and don't drink too much.'

'I won't,' he said and was gone.

'So,' her mother said, 'did you tell him?'

'I said I would.'

'And what did he say?'

'He said it was all right.'

34

It wasn't all right, though, she could tell when she came back and her dad was sitting over the kitchen fire and her mam was nowhere to be seen.

'You're late,' he said.

It wasn't late but then he was never long at the pub.

'I hear you've been out to tea,' was the first thing he said.

'Supper,' she corrected him. That was what they called it, much more exciting than tea. They had sat in the dining room and it had a big log fire and a long narrow table and there had been candles and wine and proper plates and a cloth and everything. She had never dined in style before and they had dressed up, Sir Angus in a nice suit and his sister in a nice dress though plain. 'I did tell you I was going.'

'You want nowt with folk like that, Erin,' he said.

'Rich people, do you mean?'

'He's in a bad way by what I hear.'

'Yes, he was wounded and can't go back.'

'What sort of wounded?'

Relaxing under the sound of an interested question Erin explained. Her father shook his head.

'What does he want with a bit lass like you?'

'To be friends, I expect.'

'Nay, Erin, don't be daft. Has he touched you?'

'Of course not,' she said, impatient and wishing she hadn't been so open. 'He wouldn't do such a thing. We talked about his travels. He's been everywhere.' He made it sound so exciting too, the desert, Egypt, all over Europe. Erin would have loved to travel.

'He won't be going far now, though, eh?'

Erin said nothing. He would not and it was sad.

'What about Kelvin?'

This made her feel uncomfortable, guilty. She didn't want to think about it. Kelvin was not real. He was in France. He was a nice lad and that was all. But when she went to bed she remembered Kelvin's dark eyes and the promise that she had made to him.

She spent time lying in the darkness staring up at the ceiling rehearsing the letter she would send to him. She tried to convince herself that they had not been much to each other, that it would not hurt him unduly – it had been two kisses in her mother's front room – but it was not true. She would have to accept that he would never speak to her again.

Why? It was not that she loved Angus Ballantine. How could she? He was so much older and had led a different life. It was the life he led that she had fallen in love with and she knew that she could never be happy now, that Kelvin could not make her happy, that if she stayed here and married him she would make him unhappy too. Kelvin was young, he would find somebody else, but she knew somehow that Angus would not. Having justified her actions to herself she went to sleep.

It was on the third visit, a Sunday afternoon, that Angus Ballantine asked her to marry him. They were standing in the herb garden and the pink and purple heather nearby was the only colour. She looked at him in astonishment.

'Marry me? Why would you want to do that?'

He hesitated.

'Would you at least consider it before you dismiss the idea entirely? I know I'm not much any more and probably you have other ideas—'

'I don't have any other ideas,' Erin said.

'I would have asked your father first but I wanted to discover what you thought. I don't want anybody to think that I'm presumptuous. Think about it and then if you decide that you do I could talk to him.'

Erin thought of her father, little and stout, and of Sir Angus tall and thin and how he would take up the whole of their front room somehow and she could not imagine the scene. He told her not to make up her mind but to take the week.

Erin could think of nothing else and several times on the days that followed her mother had to recall her to what they were doing and to say that she couldn't understand Erin's absentmindedness but Erin thought her mother half-knew what was happening even though no one spoke a word. Angus had asked her back the next Sunday afternoon.

'You're seeing an awful lot of these people,' her mother said. 'Don't you think you should spend Sundays here with us?'

Sunday afternoon at home, her father reading the paper, her mother darning socks and the slow way that the evening came down. The street was so quiet at that time. People did nothing on Sundays around there except go to church or chapel, eat big Sunday dinners and go for a walk if the weather was good enough. It made her want to scream with boredom. She felt as though she couldn't stand any more, as though she were being stifled, suffocated.

It was not like that at Broke Hall. There was space and the long windows took in all the light and seemed to hold it. The logs fires sang and glowed, the books glittered gold and green or gold and red in the enormous bookcases, the gardens stretched out at every side.

There was nothing small or mean about it and she could have it, be what library books called 'mistress' in such a house. She could not believe the idea that she could escape from this dreary life yet it was almost a possibility.

'I like going. You don't mind, do you?' She was irritated with herself then. Not only did she want to desert her parents, she wanted them to be pleased for her. How selfish was that?

Her mother looked at her.

'Is it him or is it the house?' she said and that was astute, Erin thought.

'Both.'

Her mother stirred in her chair.

'Erin—'

'He wants to marry me.'

There was only slight surprise in her mother's gaze but a great deal of dismay.

'I thought something of the kind. Well, I suppose it's better than what I thought he wanted but only just. Why can't you settle for a nice lad on your own level? What makes you think you'll be happy with people like that?'

'Do you think I'm happy here?' Erin said and then wished she hadn't. Her mother's face resembled wood.

'I suppose not, otherwise you wouldn't wish to be changing things.'

'Aren't people meant to better themselves?'

'It depends on what you mean by better,' her mother said.

37

'You go ahead and marry him but I think you'll rue the day.'

'Oh, Mam, try not to think badly of me. I care a lot about you and Dad but I want to do something exciting, something new.'

When her dad came in the first thing her mother said to him was, 'That man's asked our Erin to marry him.'

Her father didn't believe it, she could see. He thought it was a joke, he thought his hearing was playing him up.

'What?' he said.

'That Sir Angus Ballantine. He wants to wed our Erin.'

'Erin's marrying Kelvin,' he said, almost as though she wasn't there. 'It's all decided.'

'It can be undecided,' Erin said and brought her father's gaze to rest on her face for the first time.

'You've said you'll marry him and that's that.'

'Sir Angus is coming to see you,' Erin said.

'You've told him you'll have him, haven't you?' her father guessed.

'He insisted on seeing you but yes, as a matter of fact, I have.'

'Oh, Erin, whatever have you done?' her mother said.

'So you'd do the lad down for the sake of a big old house and half a man,' her dad said.

'He isn't half a man.'

'He's far too old for you, Erin, and he's from another class. It never works, that sort of thing. Use the brains God gave you. Why should he want to marry a lass like you?'

'Why shouldn't he?'

'It's because he's been badly hurt and no lass from his own background will have him and some men have to have a woman. How do you think he'll treat you, eh?'

'There's nothing wrong with him,' Erin said. 'He's honourable and a gentleman and he wants to marry me and there's no reason why I shouldn't.'

'There's every reason why you shouldn't, you're promised to a good God-fearing lad who's out there fighting for his country. Angus Ballantine's never done a decent day's work in his life before he went to war. He's sat on his backside and waited for other folk to do the work. People like

38

that, I cannot stick them and you are not going to marry
him.'

The little room resounded with her father's loud voice but
Erin was determined.

'I am going to marry him,' she said, 'and there's nothing
you can do to stop me,' and she ran out.

She ran all the way to Broke Hall and ran crying into the
kitchen, where Diana was making scones as usual. When she
enquired for Angus, Diana said, 'He's gone to bed to lie
down for a while. Tell me what the problem is. Maybe I can
help.'

'Angus has asked me to marry him.'

'I know. He told me.'

'My father says he won't allow it. I was . . . I had said I
would marry one of the lads from the village,' the words
came out in a rush and Diana looked dismayed.

'You'd promised that you would marry him.'

'Not exactly, no. Yes, yes, I had. But I don't want to marry
him. I want to marry Angus. Surely you're allowed to change
your mind.'

'Nobody should have to marry anybody they don't care
about.'

'He's at the Front, fighting. My father says it wouldn't be
fair and I know it's true and I promised him but I don't want
to marry him now, I really don't. This is what I want.'

'Things aren't fair,' Diana pointed out. 'Especially in war
and though it is awful to let somebody down it happens all
the time and if you married this other man it is for life and
you might regret it very much. Surely your father can see that.'

'I think all he can see is that he lost my brother in the war
and if I marry Angus he'll lose me as well in a way.'

'Yes, it is difficult,' Diana said. 'Would you like me to
come back with you and talk to your parents?'

'I don't see how that would help,' Erin said, horrified at
the idea of a woman trying to tell her father what to do and
think.

'We have no chauffeur today and Angus can't walk all
that way. You'd better stay the night and go back in the
morning.'

39

It was easy to stay the night, to have a huge room all to herself and be able to close the thick curtains at night and wake up to the sounds of the countryside, the birds in the garden. Erin loved it. She knew it was not a mistake to marry Angus. It was easier still to go straight to work from there the following day and then to go back to Broke Hall in the evening. There was still no chauffeur, he was ill, so if she went back she would have to go by herself.

She didn't go back. She went to stay at Broke Hall and even though Angus wanted to go and see her father and talk to him and urged her to get in touch with her parents she would not. She refused to let him see her parents or talk to them, she could imagine the scene in the front room in the house in Lilac Street, her father being nasty to Sir Angus and Angus having to put up with it all so there was only Erin, Angus, Diana, Mr Andrews the chauffeur and Lilian with Nora at the wedding.

She had been thinking about Lilian for some reason and thinking of her seemed to make her appear and Erin was amazed. She looked prosperous like never before, not quite so thin, happy, clear-eyed. It was the Saturday before the wedding and she was crossing the marketplace and there was Lilian, carrying the baby and seeming delighted to meet her.

She took Erin back to the house she was living in and although it was not, Erin thought, as good as the house she was about to become mistress of, it was still a lovely place with gardens below it, half a dozen imposing rooms downstairs and a big staircase which went round and round up into the darkness. They sat by Lilian's sitting-room fire and congratulated one another on their success.

'But what will you do when the war is over and Mr Armstrong comes home?' she asked Lilian.

'I'm to stay here for the time being. Mr Armstrong will live with his parents. I offered to move but he wouldn't have it and his dad has been ever so nice and gave me a job in their office and he found me a woman to take care of Nora during the week. They've been so kind to me.'

It was then that Erin asked her to come to the wedding.

Lilian said she had nobody to leave Nora with on Saturdays and Nora might cry and spoil it.

'I'd like to have somebody there for me. I've treated my mam and dad so badly over the whole thing. Please come. I don't mind if the baby cries,' Erin said so Lilian agreed.

She was glad Lilian was there. They were married in the little chapel next to the house, a tiny whitewashed place which Diana assured her had been there since the sixteen-hundreds. Erin had never seen a church anywhere near as plain with windows high up so that there was no view and the light held shadows as it fell through even in the middle of the day. The altar held no adornment. Erin carried a posy of a few flowers which Diana had gathered earlier from the rose garden across from the house. There was no music and nobody spoke after the ceremony.

It was not as Erin had ever thought her wedding would be, no guests, no celebration. Part of her wanted to run home back to Lilac Street, this was all so alien to her. She did not even have a new dress, her mother would not give her a penny of all the money she had earned and since she had given up work at the clothing factory a week before the marriage and tipped up her money to her mother without thinking about it she had, in a different way, left Lilac Street as badly off as Lilian.

After the wedding they went back to the house and drank champagne and that was when Erin began to feel less odd, and not to want to run back to her parents. As she saw Lilian and the baby away from the house she did feel lonely but only for a few seconds. She gazed around her at the gardens and then back at the way the sunshine was turning the house to gold. This was what she had wanted and now it was all hers.

The house and its gardens were the lover she had dreamed of but Angus was not. It was not his fault, it was, she hoped, nobody's fault. She felt not a spark of passion for him. She had imagined somehow that she would, that the place and the circumstances and the fact that he had married her would help, but it did not. Even now the bedroom which was theirs was cold. It was in the oldest part of the building and had small windows which looked out across the back at the ponds and the fields.

She couldn't understand why he wanted to sleep there but when she questioned him he said that his ancestors had slept in that room since twelve hundred, that the master of the house always slept there so there was obviously no argument which would help. The bedrooms in the Georgian part of the house were much prettier though much smaller. Here the room was huge and cold because it went right up into the roof without anything to stop it. She could not and did not want to imagine what it would be like in winter.

There was a big open fire of course but he said that it was never lit, there was nobody to bring in the huge amount of wood it burned and in any case the wood supply was not what it was. Like a lot of other things, Erin thought.

She felt sorry for him and she had not known that that was not the kind of thing you wanted to feel for a man you were about to go bed with.

'Come along,' Angus urged her from the depths of the bed. 'Aren't you going to undress?'

She tried to do so turned away so that he would not see her. The room was so cold once she was into the one good nightdress she owned. It was awful having to get into bed with somebody and she felt panicky and wanted to run out of the room. His body was not in good shape, it had come through too much, she had tried not to look at him but it was impossible not to notice. Now, as she cowered at her side of the bed, Angus reached for her and she had to remind herself that he was entitled to. The kissing wasn't too bad though rather wet and unpleasant and then he put his hands under her nightdress onto her body. She found him impatient with her though he apologized and tried not to be.

Equally she told herself that this had been her choice and going to bed with him was part of it. He didn't hurt her and neither did he arouse any passion in her other than the desire to run out of the room. She thought she would never want to be near anybody again if that was what it was going to be like. She had not known that men required their wives naked. No man had ever seen her naked, even her mother hadn't seen her without her clothes on since she had been very small.

When he was on top of her what she felt was shock and then disgust. He slobbered gleefully over her breasts like a sucking child and his hard hands bit into her soft flesh. Nothing happened. She didn't know what she had expected but nothing like this. If it was like this women wouldn't do it, wouldn't agree ever to do such a thing, it was so horrible.

When he released her she was relieved but when he went to sleep, which he did almost straight away, Erin was frustrated. She had never been with a man before and couldn't believe that it was like this. He lay there snoring beside her.

But the following morning as she awoke the sun was pouring in at the little windows and she dressed quickly and went outside and then she remembered why she had married him. The little gardens were bursting with flowers and the iron archways which separated the gardens were covered in honeysuckle and there was a little stream running free down the hill towards the Wear.

Further over in the main front garden she could see the towers of the cathedral, glinting in the morning light. It was all hers. She went back into the kitchen, into the gloom of the house. Diana looked shyly at her.

'Isn't it a beautiful morning?' Erin said.

'It is. Best of all the hens have laid half a dozen eggs.'

'And you've made bread, already? You must have been up hours.'

'I like to get up early. Is he awake yet?'

'I don't know.'

'You'd better go and see. He'll need a hand with washing and dressing and I'll sort out the breakfast.'

It had not occurred to Erin that she would need to help him, she did not know now what she thought. He was, in fairness, trying to help himself but it became obvious over the next half-hour that she was going to have to help him wash and dress every morning.

It was like having a child and not a husband in a way. He seemed to think nothing wrong in this. He talked as though

43

they went on like this every day. He seemed happy, he was glad they were married, she could tell. There was as much sunshine coming off him as there was coming off the room. She couldn't help thinking how much she liked him but it wasn't love.

She could see now that she would never love him. She felt about him rather like she did about her dad except that she had always known her dad and he had done his best for her and that was love in a way. This was different.

She wondered whether he would want to climb on top of her and puff and strain all to no avail every night and how unpleasant it would be. She tried to keep a sense of proportion about it. It was what wives did, they put up with their life in the bedroom for the sake of children. However, she didn't want children and she certainly didn't want this whatever it was in the bedroom.

The breakfast however was good. After that Diana needed help hoeing the vegetable patch. Erin had thought she might enjoy that but the day was hot and she was soon uncomfortable beneath the sun even with a hat on. Progress was slow and she was pleased when they sat in the shade over their lunch. It was a very basic meal such as she would have had at home, water to drink and sandwiches.

Diana baked that afternoon but Erin was required to go back to the vegetable patch and hoe again and the area seemed to get bigger and bigger. Angus was of no help, how could he be? He dozed in the shade.

There were no visitors. It was very quiet and Erin found it strange. She was used to the streets of the town but when she offered to go into town and buy anything they might need Diana laughed and said they bought nothing any more, they could not afford it.

'You live on what you grow?'

'We do, more or less. I shoot the odd rabbit or two and kill a hen when we can't get by without meat any longer.'

'You can't afford things.'

'We cannot. I can't go out and work and leave Angus. I could when you get used to dealing with him and with the house yourself of course—'

44

'Dealing with the house?'

'Everything is to do. We don't have any help. It's a full-time job managing a house like this, I can tell you. I'm never done cleaning and scrubbing and cooking and baking. The animals have to be fed twice a day, the cow milked, the fires cleaned out, the brasses are to do, such as they are, we've had to sell most of them, and there's washing and ironing and . . . all the usual things. I'm sure you did that at home.'

'I worked at the factory. Mam did all the housework.'

Diana looked hopefully at her.

'A wage would be useful. Some ready cash . . .'

'You want me to go back to work?'

'I'm used to dealing with everything here. If you'd rather stay here and do this I'm sure I could—'

'No, no,' Erin said. And then she thought of her pride at leaving, at marrying such a well-off man and how envious many of the girls had been. But it wasn't fair to Diana or Angus that she should not try to help. She would go back.

'I'll go and ask for my job straight away,' she said and she looked at the vegetable patch and thought that she quite liked this really, you could see exactly where you had been and you got to eat the results of your labour. She had never done anything like that before and it looked so neat and so clean that she was pleased with her day's work.

That night Angus pinned her to the bed again and sweated and strained and Erin was not sure she could endure it. It was not that he hurt her but she was embarrassed and uncomfortable and his flesh seemed so old and crêped and used up.

He was so grateful to her, she thought, and she knew then that this was what he had married her for, so that he could feel her naked body under him and apply his hot wet mouth and heavy hands to various parts of her body.

He pretended not to hear her when she asked him to stop and when she tried to turn away he pleaded with her in a childish voice and called her silly baby names until she was so embarrassed her face was burning.

In the end she gave in and then she thought he was taking longer and longer each night to bring his body to that final shuddering sticky disgusting finish on her stomach which had nothing whatsoever to do with her. Worse was to follow and she was convinced that respectable people did not do the things that he asked her to do. She was revolted by the taste and feel of him.

She went back to the factory and asked for her job. Nobody said anything, nobody seemed surprised to see her or asked about her marriage. Things went on there as usual, there was after all still a war on, but the rumours were that it would soon be over. There had been rumours for years but this time they were more substantial, this time the war was really going to end and she could not help being as happy as everybody else was.

After she had been married for two weeks she couldn't stand being away from her parents any longer. On the Sunday afternoon therefore when it was rainy and Angus had fallen asleep and Diana was messing about with the baking in the kitchen she walked across town.

She paused when she reached Lilac Street and thought she had never imagined she would be pleased to go back there. She walked up the yard and opened the door and her mother looked up from where she too was baking, her face red from the oven heat. Her mother looked hard at her and then her eyes filled with tears and she said, 'Oh, Erin, I'm so glad you came,' and she went over and took Erin into her embrace for the first time in years and her dad came out of the front room.

Erin cried and said how sorry she was for what she had done and her dad cuddled her and he smiled and looked so relieved that Erin was full of joy.

They sat over the kitchen fire and ate jam tarts as soon as the jam was cool enough to be eaten and her mam gave her hot tea and they talked and her dad said how glad he was to see her and he asked after Angus and Diana and Erin was happier then than she had been in a long time.

'I've gone back to the factory,' Erin said. She had to tell them, they would find out from other people. Their response surprised her. She thought they would think it shameful for her to work when she was married to a well-heeled man.

46

'Well done, Erin,' her mother said. 'It doesn't do for folk to get above themselves and everybody has to help during a war. I think it's every credit to you.'

'We need the money.'

'Everybody needs more money,' her father said.

She was reluctant to leave and go back. She was so late that Angus was already in bed. She hoped that he would be asleep but he was not and eager for her.

'Do we have to do this every night?' she said gently when he reached for her.

'No, of course not.'

'I would rather we didn't if you don't mind. I think I'm about to have my period and I get cramps.'

It wasn't a lie, she was due to bleed, but she felt awful when he said, 'You can do what I want without me going anywhere near you.'

'I can't.'

'Oh yes, you can. It's your duty as my wife to attend to my needs.'

'I don't like doing that.'

'Yes, you do,' he said and pushed her head down insistently.

Erin thought it would not be long before she hated him.

Six

Many of the men who had gone to war and survived were a long time coming home. Kelvin was lucky, he was one of the first to come back. It was well after the turn of the year by the time he reached Durham. The truth of the matter was, he thought, as he got off the train, that his hopes had died along with a lot of other things, in France. He knew he should have been grateful to come back but he wasn't. He still had the letter which Erin had written to him almost a year and a half since saying that she was going to marry another man. Because of it he could not go back to the street where at first he had assumed she was waiting for him.

He did not feel as though he had any place there nor that her parents would be expecting him back there now that he was not about to become their son-in-law. Kelvin had never felt so completely alone. Erin had robbed him not just of herself and their marriage but a place, a family, some roots. There was nobody for him. He longed to see them, to be told it had all been a dreadful mistake and Erin was waiting for him.

In the end he went to the nearest hotel after he had walked away from the station and down towards North End, the Garden House. He shouldn't really have gone to a hotel but it was on the edge of the town and he felt less likely to see anybody he knew.

He could actually afford it, he thought, thinking cynically of his finances. There had been nobody to support, nothing to give his wages to for years. He didn't have to worry for a long while, which was just as well, he thought, after the first couple of days. There was very little work to be had and hundreds of men were returning home to the area.

One night they were short-handed in the bar. He ended up helping out because he was bored and offered and after that they kept him on and gave him room and food for nothing and it was a great deal more than many people had though he had to move to one of the attic rooms and be available all day to help in the kitchen. He liked it. It stopped the loneliness.

He had been there several weeks when Erin's dad, Arthur, appeared mid-evening. Arthur looked as though he felt out of place. He always drank at the same place, his local at Heath Houses, and this was not it.

At first Kelvin couldn't understand what Arthur was doing all the way across town, it was a good hour's walk, and then he understood. Arthur knew he was there. He came straight up to the bar and said, 'I want a word with you.'

'I'm working.'

'When you're ready. In the meanwhile I'll have a pint.'

Kelvin served him and then as Arthur sat down he thought he might as well get it over with so as he was due a break he asked if he could go and sit with him and the manager said it was all right. He went. Arthur was by the window.

It was a good view across open ground beyond the road and in a tree at the far side Kelvin could see a jay. It had the appearance of a magpie but with grey and brown plumage. It was so pretty, he thought, but then everything seemed so. He was only just beginning to believe that the war was over and that he might go on living for a considerable time. It was a strange and rather wonderful idea.

'You didn't come and see us,' Arthur said. 'We understand why but we wish you had. I didn't even know you were back. You could have come, no matter what the circumstances.'

'I didn't want to. I thought Erin wouldn't want me there.'

'It isn't like that.' Arthur looked straight at him. 'She had her head turned. In a way you can't blame her – well, maybe you can, but we find it difficult. She always had ideas, she was always reading and dreaming and . . . the war was hard for people in different ways. She was never the same after our John died.' Arthur's gaze faltered at that point and he

49

looked down for a few moments. 'None of us was, that's the truth. She'd always been a good lass but I think we neglected her and she got sick of it and went off.'

'War does funny things to people,' Kelvin said.

'Aye. I'm sorry. We badly wanted you as a son-in-law, we're disappointed people in almost every way. The worst of it is I don't think our Erin is happy. If she'd married and been happy we would have lived with it.'

'Things never work out the way you think they're going to,' Kelvin said.

Arthur looked at him again. 'Come and stay with us.'

'I've got a job here.'

'You can keep the job on if it's what you want—'

'It isn't what I want. It was all I could get at the time.'

'Come and stay anyhow. Sadie said I wasn't to come back until you'd agreed.'

'I can't.'

'Because of Erin? She hardly ever comes, I wish she would more. I don't think she wants us to know she isn't happy. He's too old for her but she wouldn't be bid and I think she knows it now and . . . he can't see and . . . he can't walk very far and . . . it can't be much fun for a young lass being married to somebody like that. I'm not saying you should see her, I think that might be downright bad for both of you, but I wouldn't let any ideas like that stop you from coming back to Lilac Street. It's your home and we want you there.'

It was the handsomest thing anybody had ever said to Kelvin and reminded him that he was lonely. He had just pushed it to the back of his mind because he was busy. He wanted to go back there, he wanted to be among the people he had known as a child. He thought if he went back he might find something which he had lost and not just Erin. He didn't know what it was exactly but it had to be better than this.

He went to see them the next day and Mrs Marsden greeted him with tea and cake and urged him to go back and live with them.

'I can't. I have to stay there if I want to keep my job.'

50

'It would be like having our John back,' she said. That wasn't quite what she meant but he knew.

'I have to have work. I can't live off you.'

'Arthur is being made deputy. I'm sure he could help,' she said, swelling with pride rather at her husband's promotion.

'Is that right?' Kelvin said.

'Aye, it is,' her husband said. 'So come back, eh?'

He moved in at the end of the week and was happier than he had been since he had received the letter from Erin. Arthur managed to get him a job hewing and the security and safety of being in their home almost like their son played well on his mind. He began to sleep properly for the first time in years. He even put on weight and went out to the pub with Arthur and his friends.

He dreaded seeing Erin again but thought about her all the time and the letter she had sent him which he kept. He didn't know why he kept it. In a way if it had been an offhand kind of note he could have stood it better but Erin had tried to explain herself and told him how sorry she was and how afraid she had been that he would not come back and then she would be left in Lilac Street with her parents forever and nobody would ever marry her.

He didn't understand how such a beautiful lass could think such a thing but then she always had been afraid of being left. She told him that she would never love Angus as she loved him but she couldn't turn down the opportunity for such a life. She hoped he wouldn't think too badly of her.

He wished he could throw it away but he didn't seem able to, as though it was all he had left of her, her thin pretty handwriting on the single white sheet where she announced with a pride she couldn't help that she was about to marry Sir Angus Ballantine, some upper-class man. The longest part of the letter was where she talked about the beautiful house which Angus owned in Durham and that was when Kelvin understood.

She had given him up for a house with a big garden and her idea of the life that it would provide. It had always been one of her dreams when she was a little girl, that she would get away and live in a fairy-tale castle. He thought about

51

Heath Houses, about Lilac Street and how often when he was cold and wet and longed for home he had pictured them playing in the back lane as children, he and John playing conkers while Erin and the other girls sang skipping games. He thought of them sitting on the back step by the gate as people went by.

His dad had been alive and the summers had seemed long and warm and the older people sat out in their back yards on crackets or kitchen chairs and read and smoked and gossiped. Erin had always made up stories about getting away, going over the sea to different countries and living another kind of life. He had thought she was daft.

It seemed to him that Lilac Street was the most precious place on earth and he had longed to go back to it, the familiar shops, the Methodist chapel, the pit head and the road which wound into Durham and from which after you had walked a little way beyond the village you could see the cathedral. It had always been so comforting.

Unlike millions of other men, he had got home at last and found some peace, but he dreaded meeting her, he dreaded how he missed her, longed for her, was desperate with loneliness and boredom because she wasn't there and he realized then that you couldn't live with any degree of joy without somebody you loved.

The time stretched out before you a long road that you plodded wearily along, so much as he dreaded seeing her he dreaded not seeing her so much more, lived for even the idea of five minutes in her company.

Seven

'We're going to have to sell the house,' Angus announced one cold day in early spring.

They were sitting in the dining room. It was so cold that Erin couldn't concentrate on anything. They were used to it but she had never encountered anything like the cold in that house, she could not sleep at night because of it, she could not think about anything but how she would like to sit over the drawing-room fire for the next four months until the weather warmed up a bit.

'Sell it?' she said. What on earth did he mean? The house was the only joyful thing of their existence, it was all there was left, she worked for it every day, put up with him every night.

'We've run out of money.'

'Long since,' Diana said with a sigh.

'And now that the war's over surely somebody will want to buy it. It's a good house, it's been in the family all this time.'

'You can't sell it, it's been in the family for hundreds of years,' Erin protested.

'We don't have any choice.'

'We have my wage.'

He smiled at her.

'I know, and you've done very well, but it doesn't keep us, it doesn't begin to. A house like this has a big mouth and . . .'

'You can't sell it,' she said. 'You can't possibly do that. I won't let you.'

He looked surprised.

'Erin, I know you love it, I'm glad you have such affection

53

for it, but we can no longer survive here. We have very little to eat, we have no money for fuel. It's our only remaining asset. We have to find a buyer for it.'

Erin could not think what it would be like when she had nothing left. All that mattered was the house. The car had been sold and that had helped for a while and there was no chauffeur to pay and she had not cared so very much about it, just the pride she had felt at them having a car.

She went to work five days a week. Now that the war was over the clothing factory had gone on to making men's suits and they were doing very well but she was bored with the work and with having nothing to come back to but a meagre dinner and no entertainment, nothing but huddling over the fire until she was tired, listening to Diana reading to her brother and then going into a freezing room to put up with a man who had begun to smell and feel old and wanted her to do disgusting acts, it was not to be borne.

At least he had stopped asking if he could touch her most of the time. Very occasionally she let him, she suffered him and even he had stopped pretending that there was any enjoyment in it.

Sometimes she thought he regretted their marriage very much but they were polite to one another, nobody said anything, they went on from day to day. She thought she would go mad if she had to go on without the house.

'We can't move from here, we just can't,' she said.

'Erin, we have to,' Diana put in and that was when Erin got up from the table and ran away, crying like somebody much younger, she thought in disgust at herself.

That night after work she could not bring herself to go home, she thought of it as home. She felt certain it was the place that she was meant to be. She went instead to Lilac Street.

Her dad was not yet back from work and her mam was seeing to the supper and then the back door clashed and when Erin turned around there stood Kelvin. He had obviously come back from the pit and washed and changed. His hair was still wet and he was in his shirtsleeves. He looked so young. The weariness of the war had fallen away from him.

'Lady Ballantine,' he said, 'and how are we today?'

54

Through the open door Erin was aware of her mother as she went on with her kitchen tasks, not speaking and not even raising her head. Her father returned and he washed the pit dirt away and then they sat down to eat.

Kelvin barely spoke all the way through the meal. She couldn't think of anything to say. Afterwards she helped her mother to wash up, her father said he was going to the pub. He invited Kelvin to go with him but the younger man just shook his head. Her mother went next door with a plate of dinner for Florrie Smith, who was poorly.

Kelvin didn't look at her. He looked as though he was about to run out of the house but he didn't go. Erin stared out of the window at the neatness of the back yard with its tin bath hanging up on one side and its lavatory and coal house. She should make an excuse and leave but somehow she couldn't.

Kelvin didn't help, he didn't say anything, just stretched out his long legs in front of him and gazed into the fire, for somewhere to look, she thought.

'I'm sorry,' Erin said.

'Sorry?' His eyes were scornful. 'You think that mends it, do you?'

Erin, used to a middle-aged disabled man, could not help admiring the youth and strength of him, Angus was not well enough to loose his temper on anybody. Kelvin had no such problem, his green eyes glinted.

'I don't know what to say to you,' Erin said

'There's nowt you can say.'

'I just . . .'

'He turned your head with his money and his title and his . . . big house.'

'I suppose you could say that.'

'Aye, I would.'

Erin didn't know how to make a reply, she felt like crying. He looked across the kitchen fire and she thought his green eyes were so beautiful and he said, 'I'd like to make you sorry,' as though it were a threat.

'But I am.'

'Are you? You gave me up for a blind, lame man and his bloody house. You – you disloyal little cow.'

55

Kelvin, she thought, had learned new words in France and his eyes were the colour of the waves off Seaham beach on a stormy day. She thought they had never been so intense, so lit. He looked as though he wanted to hit her though of course he wouldn't. She knew he wouldn't.

'You shouldn't say things like that to me.'

'You going to stop me, are you?'

She could feel the restraint coming off him and all of a sudden she thought what it would be like to be in bed with him and not Angus and it made her blush. Somehow she managed to convey her embarrassment. Kelvin looked away.

She realized then for the first time that sex was meant to be exciting, that that was the whole point of it, the real reason people married, to try and put a barrier around something which otherwise might not be contained. She was amazed. She had not thought she would ever think positively about something which was so awful.

The whole room was stilled and even though Kelvin didn't touch her or look at her she wanted him so much that her breath was uneven. How terrible. She had not known before then that Angus had taught her how things were meant to be, how they were not with him but could be with another man. All the things she lacked she knew about.

She was disgusted with herself and her husband. She didn't see how she could bear to spend another night with him and then she understood what she had done to herself and to Kelvin. They could have had a happy life together and she had ruined it with greed.

Erin was so ashamed of herself that she wanted to cry which prevented her from speaking. The fairy tale had turned into a nightmare and it was nobody's fault but hers. She did not think that Angus had ever told her he was rich, the illusion had been in her mind. She had made a mess of things but then he was selfish and demanding and she disliked him so much now that it made her feel sick.

'I'm ever so sorry,' she said and then she left as fast as she could.

* * *

56

That night lying beside Angus while he slept, breathing deeply and snoring a little from time to time, she could not stop thinking about Kelvin McCormack. Had he always looked as good as that and she had just taken him for granted or was it just that he now had a second chance at life and was determined to be optimistic and make the best of it?

The following evening she very much wanted to go back to Lilac Street but she made herself go home and it was the same routine, rabbit, vegetables, custard pie. Diana complained because the hens had stopped laying and these were the last of the eggs.

There was so little fuel the only fire burning now was in the kitchen which did for cooking, washing and heating and they had taken to sitting in there. The following day she came home early and the fire was not on in there and she guessed that Diana had taken to putting it on in the late afternoon so that they could have relatively comfortable evenings.

The next day was Saturday and she would be required to help with the household chores. That afternoon she made an excuse and went to her parents' house. She walked in and there was no one about. The house was silent.

She went through into the front room. The fire burned in there and it was a proper coal fire, her father had a coal allowance as all the pitmen did, the house was always warm. Kelvin was lying on the sofa. He sat up when she came into the room as though he had been almost asleep.

'Oh hello,' he said and his voice was soft and throaty and his eyes were like green glass. 'Your dad's out and your mam's . . . she's gone to spend some time with Florrie. I think she's getting worse. She very often goes there during the afternoons. You all right?'

'Grand,' Erin said, holding her hands out to the blaze.

'You don't seem it.'

She glanced into his sympathetic face.

'Angus is selling the house. At least when he can find a buyer. His family has lived there for eight hundred years. Can you imagine?'

'Not really. It must be funny for your family to live anywhere for that long.'

'Do you think?'

'You don't want to leave?'

'Of course I don't want to leave. I love that house. Mind you, it's the coldest place in creation at the moment. I wish the summer was here.'

'Where will you go?'

'I don't know. We haven't talked about it. He has no money, you see, and he can't work. I'm the only worker in our house.'

'That must be hard.'

'Not really. I suppose I should be grateful.'

'For what?'

Indeed. That was it. Nobody ever came to the house. They seemed to have no friends. There was no decent food left. There was no joy. There was nothing but work, which went on and on.

'A lot of people have a lot less,' she said.

'Do they?'

When she didn't answer he said, 'Do you love him, then?'

Erin stared into the fire.

'I thought I did,' she said.

'But you're too young to love somebody like that?'

She glanced at him, amazed at the understanding.

'It was the house I loved. Isn't that awful?'

'No, it's . . . understandable, I think.'

'I want . . . I just want . . .'

Kelvin leaned over and he got hold of her and kissed her. It was exactly what she wanted to do. His mouth was soft and gentle and he smelled so young and clean.

'Don't.'

He did it again and when she protested and tried to get away he held her, he must have known she didn't want to get away and though she tried to make herself not want him it was impossible. She was just so pleased when he pulled her down on the sofa on top of him and into his arms and then he kissed her as she thought she had always wanted somebody to kiss her.

He tasted so fresh and so young and so sweet and although her mind told her that this was a betrayal, that Angus didn't deserve she should carry on with somebody else, she lost control of her body completely. She let him put his hands under her cardigan, in spite of the fact that she was convinced her mother would come in at any second.

After that first on the sofa and then on the floor she let him put his hands all over her and it was nothing like her experience of such things. She wanted him to touch her, she wanted him to go on and on kissing her, she liked it when he pulled her clothes off her and although her face burned with embarrassment she couldn't stop him from placing his knee between her thighs and after that it was quite different from anything that Angus had ever achieved. It hurt. He seemed surprised, hesitated even at her drawn-in breath.

'You all right, Erin?'

She didn't say anything.

'Do you want me to stop?'

The tears were running down her face.

'Yes. No. No, I don't.'

'Are you sure? I'm not a dog, you know. I can control myself.' There was a hint of humour and it made the situation so much easier. She looked at him, smiled at his concerned face.

'I love you,' he said. 'I've always loved you but I wouldn't hurt you, not for anything. You're another man's wife and—'

'I loved you too,' Erin said, almost crying. 'I always have done, I was just too stupid to know. Do it.'

It was the most uncomfortable thing that had ever happened to her and she was not surprised that Angus hadn't managed it. It took a lot of energy and even though Kelvin was as gentle as he could be, she thought, it was still an aggressive thing to do. So this was what men made such a fuss about. How awful.

When she had put up with it until he didn't want her to put up with it any more it was very messy and there was blood and she wanted to cry. She would have run from the room but she wasn't sure she could run, she ached so much.

Even worse somehow he looked . . . how did he look, when she managed a shy glance? He looked horrified.

'Was there something wrong with it?' she enquired caustically. Did it hurt him too?

59

'You never did it before.'

'I have, lots of times. It never hurt before. Maybe you're doing it wrong.'

'I don't think so,' Kelvin said. 'I mean . . . it's not what you'd call complicated, is it?'

'I don't know. Isn't it? Is it always like that with you?'

Kelvin looked embarrassed.

'I don't know. I haven't done it much. Maybe I'm just not very good at it.'

'You can say that again,' Erin said and she turned away and retrieved her clothes.

And then he got hold of her while she cried and told him not to and that was when it was different. It was good like cake and beer and laughter and she had not known until then how much she wanted to be with him, with somebody young. He was kind and held her in his arms and spoke softly into her ear and nobody interrupted and the day became magical.

She got used to the presence and the feel of him. Their bodies matched and were right together. There was on his part too a certain triumph, a glee, a showing her that she could have married him and it would have been like this. It was not quite fair that he did it like that, she thought, like somebody in complete control while her own control broke down under it somehow.

Angus could never have made her want him like this. Kelvin reduced her to pleasure there on her mother's kitchen floor. She was ashamed, in fear that her mother would come back at any second, and then finally she was satisfied. And there in the silence with nothing but the coals shifting slightly in the grate he said scornfully, 'All right that time, was it?' and he moved and fastened up his clothes just as though it hadn't been important. He knew what her marriage to Angus was like without her telling him.

By the time her mam came back they were dressed and sitting on the sofa. She left almost immediately but he followed her down the yard and there she cried and said, 'I've never been so ashamed of myself. What am I doing?'

'I'm sorry. I've thought about you night and day, and I love you. It's my only excuse. I wouldn't hurt you, Erin. It

60

won't happen again. You go back home and forget about it and about me. I'll go away.'

'You do that,' Erin said, desperate to hurt him and then she ran away. She ran all the way home.

The trouble was that somehow she couldn't resist going back to the house when she was almost sure of finding him by himself but her mam and dad were both there so when she left all that happened was that she and Kelvin stood in the shadows by the corner and he kissed her and the more he kissed her the more she wanted him.

'I don't want you to go away,' Erin said and she clung and kissed him.

Walking back home, she thought of how very much she loved him and it was terrifying. She must never see him on her own again. She must encourage him to go away. They must not meet.

The following day when she came out of work in the darkness he was there and he stepped from the shadows as she lingered when everybody had gone and she kissed him and when he walked her across Framwellgate Bridge and up North Road and into the Garden House Hotel she did not think to say no. There he procured a room, he knew one of the people who helped behind the bar, and they went up the back stairs and there in the quietness they went to bed.

Part of it was because she shouldn't. Part of it was because Angus and Diana were waiting for her at Broke Hall and part of it was to punish whoever was responsible for the idea that she could lose the house, that she could be put out like she wasn't good enough to be there.

She wanted to make some kind of a statement against it and this, she thought, was the stupid way in which she did so. She knew how stupid it was but it was all she had. It was the only drug she could find, his body and the time and the noise going on down below them as the drinkers and darts players gathered.

She knew that Kelvin didn't care any more. That his friends had been killed, his youth wasted. What did it matter to him that she was married, that this could come to nothing? He had learned that there was nothing but now, that you could

61

die at any second. There was so little left, why should they not take what they could?

She wanted to tell him that she didn't love him because it was too difficult for both of them but he smothered her in kisses and besides how inappropriate it would have been when he was giving himself here like there was no tomorrow. There wasn't and Kelvin had long since worked it out.

This time it didn't hurt and better than that she liked it as she had liked nothing before except her feeling for Broke Hall when she first saw it and the taste of the wine she got with her dinner on special occasions. She liked how Kelvin had a lot of strength and energy, she liked to give herself up to him and she found that it made her feel like somebody else, somebody she had never met before.

She wanted him to touch and kiss her, she wanted him in her more and more somehow, like some kind of drug. The excitement was amazing. It made her head spin. It made her body crave and crave him. She couldn't get enough. They stayed there for hours.

He walked her back down the road and into the town and along by the river and even then she clung and kissed him. They parted before the gates of her home. Home. It would not be that for much longer.

'How will you feel when you have nothing but him?' Kelvin said.

'What do you mean?'

'When you don't have the house any more?'

She didn't answer.

'We could go away somewhere.'

'We couldn't do that.'

He laughed.

'Why not? What difference does it make? What would you be staying for? Your parents don't need you, they have each other. I need you. I love you.'

'Kelvin . . .'

'What? Come away with me. Let's get out of here.'

'I can't leave.'

'Of course you can.' When she hesitated Kelvin said, 'He's too old for you and too ill.'

'It isn't like I thought it was going to be but that's no reason for me to give up. He's a good man and Diana is very nice and they need me.'

'Is that right? What kind of a life are you going to have?'

'I can't go on seeing you,' she said and ran away.

'Wednesday,' he called after her.

It became an addiction. She thought at first that the more she saw him the less she would want to see him but it was not so. They spent their free time in a little back bedroom at the Garden House and she lived for the meetings all that spring and summer. Her favourite time was the evenings when she dared to stay with him, all the windows open and the noises from the city far off and their bodies sweaty from the closeness of the room as they shared a cigarette and talked in low voices about what it would be like when they left, when they ran away.

In between times she would scuttle back to Angus, go to work each day and try to pretend that she was doing nothing wrong.

It was a while before Angus realized things were not as they should be and she was not surprised that he noticed. She stopped him from coming near her in bed, wouldn't do anything he wanted and even when he pleaded and begged she refused. When he tried to force her to do so she threatened him that she would go and sleep somewhere else and after that he gave in, stopped asking, so that very soon all they had was conversation.

It was the very opposite of what she had with Kelvin. Kelvin urged her to leave and she began to think that it was the best thing to do. She had no life left and although he had not sold the house yet he was obviously going to.

That autumn Kelvin urged her to run away with him until finally she said that she would, that she would talk to Angus, but she knew that she could not leave the house, that she only said that to keep Kelvin quiet, and then she came back one evening to find Angus waiting for her in the library and he had a grave look on his face.

'We've sold the house.'

She wanted to shriek and shout at him that he couldn't do that, he couldn't do anything of the kind, that it was her only reason for staying here. She didn't have to.

'It was the house you married me for,' he said. 'I'm sorry we've come to this.'

'That's not true at all. I'm very fond of you.'

He laughed but in a bitter way.

'You can't sell it,' she said. 'This is our home.'

'I'm to sign the contract tomorrow and we must look for somewhere to rent, somewhere small, and for the first time in our lives we will have some money.'

'I don't want money. I want to stay here. I love this house. It's very important to me. Please, Angus, don't sell it. I can't bear to think that we might have to leave.'

'We must. You'll get used to it.'

'Used to it?' She could feel the anger surge up inside her. 'You think I would stay with you in some awful little house?'

'You're my wife. You'll do as I say.'

She laughed.

'Whatever gave you that idea?'

'We're married. There's nothing you can do about it.'

'Oh, isn't there? If you sign that contract I will leave.'

He gazed in her direction and she felt no pity that he couldn't see. All she could think of was the panic that enveloped her at the idea of having to leave the only magical place she had ever found.

'You can't leave me, you have nowhere to go.'

'Oh yes I have. And I have someone to go with.'

'That's ridiculous.'

'No, it isn't. I have a young man, the boy I was going to marry, the one I gave up for you. I didn't realize how much I was giving up but if you sell this house I will run away with him. Then what will you do?'

'I love you, Erin, you're all I have.'

'You have Diana.'

'It isn't the same thing. Give him up, whoever he is.'

'I can't.'

'We'll be able to buy another house, something small, something easier to deal with and we'll have money. You won't have to work any more. We can spend plenty of time in one another's company and make this right.'

'It's never going to be right,' she said. 'I'm leaving you. I'm going tonight. I'm not going to waste any more of my time here with you. I don't love you. I never loved you and now I despise you and I don't want to be with you in some horrible shoddy little house. I'm going.'

'I'll never let you go,' Angus said, trying to grab her as she moved back. 'Never. How could you be unfaithful to me with some common little pitman?'

She would have turned away but he managed to find her, to get hold of her and they were beside the desk and he opened the desk drawer at the top in the middle and took a tiny silver pistol out of it. She was horrified.

'You aren't going anywhere,' he said. 'I'll kill you first. I'll kill us both.'

She tried frantically to get away from him. They struggled. His grip on her arm was savage. She kicked and punched him and twisted and turned and as her elbow landed in his stomach Angus let go of his breath in pain. She felt hatred for what he had done to her and to the house. He had not cared for how she felt or that she was young. He had thought of nothing but his own needs and desires.

And all she could think after that was that he could not sell the house. It was the only thing left which really mattered to her, the only thing in the whole world that was still precious. She really felt as though she could kill him, as though he would never let her go. He would sell the house and she would have nothing otherwise. The house was the most important thing in her life.

The panic rose. She would die, Angus would murder her right here in the library of the house that she loved so much and then she would never get out of here. She pushed, shoved him from her with a great weight of effort and for the first time she made some impact and it seemed that she had freed herself from him, got away. All she had to do was turn and run from the library, run away to Kelvin and they would leave Durham and nobody would ever know where they had gone. They would never come back.

He caught her just as she would have moved beyond his grasp and she gave an almighty push to free herself completely. The gun went off, the noise of it was huge, and then his grasp fell away from her and he was falling and the gun was falling and the sound of him falling went on and on in her mind for days and days afterwards. He was a big man, he went down hard, there was nothing to stop him but the stone fireplace and he fell back against it and his head split open like ripe fruit.

It replayed in her mind over and over but he was down on the floor and she was not and then there was blood everywhere. She got down and picked up the gun. At that moment the door opened and there, when she looked around, stood Diana, her face ghastly white, her eyes full of disbelief.

Eight

Erin had never been in a police station before in her life. All she wanted was to run back to Lilac Street and the life she had led before she had met Angus Ballantine. This could not be happening. It was a nightmare. She was taken into a dark little room and questioned about what had happened and a man called Mr Saunders, a solicitor apparently, was there too. He explained to her what would happen, that there would be a coroner's court and then possibly a trial.

'But I didn't do it,' she said blankly to him.

There seemed nothing else to say. She had not killed Angus, he had done it himself. It was all a mistake and she wanted to go home. Mr Saunders urged her to say nothing.

The police wanted to know everything about her life, what it had been like before she married, whether she had been happy in her marriage, whether Angus had behaved badly towards her. She said as little as possible because Mr Saunders had advised her not to and then from sentence to sentence she could not remember what they had said, only that they shouted and bullied her and she was upset and kept crying and the police station was so frightening and she seemed to have nobody on her side but this solicitor, whom she didn't know.

She could not believe that Angus was dead. She wanted to go back to Broke Hall and have tea and have Diana and Angus there and for everything to be normal instead of which she felt shocked, horrified, unable to say or do anything, just stuttering and faltering and having the police fall on each word and take her back over what had happened again and again.

They put her into a tiny freezing cell, dark and silent, the kind of place you might be forgotten until you died, she thought, shuddering.

'Do I have to stay here?'

'Don't worry,' Mr Saunders said. 'We'll get some help.'

Allan Jamieson was sitting with his feet up against the window ledge in his chambers just off Palace Green when Mr Roscommon, his clerk, brought Felix Saunders into his room.

'I'm not taking on anything big at the moment,' Allan said, turning around to the desk and them. 'I told Roscommon to tell you. There are plenty of decent barristers in the city, Felix, and they'll all want it, Angus Ballantine being rich and well known and a war hero.'

'Then why don't you want it?' Mr Saunders said. 'What have you got on?'

'Very little,' Roscommon said.

'Fred . . .'

'Well, you haven't, Mr Jamieson,' Mr Roscommon said with decision. 'Look at you. You've got nothing to do.'

'I can't,' Allan said.

'Just go and see her, please,' Felix said.

'It's unethical for you—'

'Are you going to sit there for the rest of your life when people need you?' Mr Saunders said. 'You were the best.'

'Yes, was,' Allan said.

'Will you live with yourself when somebody less competent defends that girl and they hang her?' Felix said.

Allan looked carefully at him.

'You think she did it? She hasn't admitted it—'

'Of course she hasn't.'

'But you think she did it?' Allan persisted.

'I think it's possible.'

That silenced the room.

'With reason?'

Saunders looked back at him, levelly.

'Nobody ever came out of the assizes happy with their neck intact because they had good reason, especially not a woman.'

'If it wasn't planned, if it was the heat of the moment, any competent barrister might get her off.'

'I want you to go and see her. Please, Allan.'

'Have they got her locked up?'

'They'll have to release her within hours and I'm going to go and hopefully get her out—'

'They shouldn't keep her in there, it isn't right if she's never done anything before.'

'This will all take weeks.'

'Has she done anything before?' Allan persisted, interested by now.

'Nothing.'

'Well, then, it shouldn't be too difficult, even for you.'

Felix smiled in acknowledgement of the backhanded compliment.

'Does that mean you'll take the case?'

'No.'

'But you'll go and see her?'

Allan hesitated, looked at the two concerned faces in front of him.

'All right, I'll see her,' he said.

When Mr Roscommon had shown Mr Saunders out he came back into the room. Allan looked at him.

'That was all deeply unethical, Fred,' Allan said.

Mr Roscommon, who hated familiarity, even with the office doors closed, winced.

'You're a manipulative man, Roscommon,' Allan said.

'Yes, sir.'

Nine

Her mother cried when Erin came in at the back door with her dad. Never had Erin thought she would be so pleased to be back in Lilac Street. Or to see her mother crying over her.

'What have they tried to do to you, Erin?' her mother said.

It was some moments before Erin thought that her mam meant Sir Angus and his sister and not the police. Her mother hugged her, sat her down, gave her tea.

'What were the police thinking of that a daughter of ours could do such a thing,' her father raged and her mother nodded. She was so very relieved to be there. The world, which had turned into a very strange place, was normal again, at least for a little while.

Kelvin came in shortly afterwards but it was all she could do to look at him. When her parents were safely in bed downstairs he came into her room. He stood by the bottom of the bed looking almost ghostly in the candlelight and said in a hoarse voice, 'What went wrong?'

Erin was incoherent with tears. She shook her head. Kelvin came over and sat on the bed and attempted to take her into his arms. She turned away. He moved back.

'What happened?' he said.

She didn't speak for several seconds. She couldn't.

'I would have come to the police station but—'

'No. You couldn't. You were right not to come. That would have been wrong and foolish. You mustn't be involved at all. If anybody were to find out . . . about you I'd be finished.'

She could not believe the words even as she said them.

'But you didn't kill him,' Kelvin said, 'you couldn't have.'

'No.' Even as she said it she wasn't sure. She had been so angry with him, so hurt, so . . . 'I didn't mean anything.'

Kelvin looked blankly at her.

'You did it? You couldn't have. You don't have a gun, you don't know how to use one—'

'He got it from the drawer.'

'He had a gun?'

'A little silver pistol. He was angry with me—'

'Had you told him about us?'

Had she? She couldn't be sure now.

'No, no, I don't think so, not . . . not specifically. I told him I didn't want him to sell the house and that if he sold it I would leave him and he was so angry.'

'Was he trying to shoot you?'

'Me or himself. I'm not certain now. I tried to stop him. There was a struggle. He fell and banged his head on the hearth and then . . . so much blood.'

'I can't believe this has happened,' Kelvin said. 'It wasn't your fault, it can't have been.'

'I should never have married him.'

'You weren't to know.'

'I should have. You know I should have,' she said. 'You'd better go back into your own room, I don't want my parents to be suspicious and they might hear us through the floor.'

'I want us to be together.'

'We can't. Not at the moment. We have to pretend. If we make a mistake now I won't live through this trial. We mustn't be seen together. If anyone were to find out . . . You should move out.'

He looked at her.

'I don't want to.'

'I know you don't want to and I don't want you to but I think you should. You don't have to go far. Mrs Connors in Camellia Street has a spare room. We could still see each other a bit and you could still come to the house but it must look very respectable and we need to have that for the time being.'

Kelvin tried to take her into his arms.

'No,' she said, 'we mustn't.'

71

Ten

It was raining. Allan watched the drops running in long lines down the dining-room windows. It was dark outside but inside were dozens of candles, Kaye loved them and placed them so that they reflected in the mirrors in each room and lit the windows, lit the rain. He had watched the rain in France for so long so often that he thought it seemed different here, closer to you somehow, though he couldn't think why. He missed the rain in France. Four long years of war, months before he got home, nearly all his friends killed and every misery conceivable inflicted upon the men and yet he missed it.

This seemed unreal. It was Saturday night and Kaye had insisted on a dinner party. He couldn't think why, only that he had agreed. He had spent most of the day at his chambers beside Palace Green within the shadow of the great cathedral and there he had lingered, imagining Kaye's friends arriving, how bright she would be, wearing a new dress and saying he had been delayed, he would surely not be long and he had made himself go home, dress up, act the part.

They were her friends, he had hardly anybody left. All hers seemed to have survived. Even her bloody obnoxious brother, Reginald. He couldn't go to war of course, he wasn't fit enough. Good old Reggie, the kind of man who could spend money but was too damned stupid to imagine how he might earn any. Reggie was almost amusing, always drunk, always in funds. His father being long dead, Jake's father kept him. Your uncle's wallet, Allan thought, the last refuge of the terminally immature.

Agnes and Freddie Smithson were there. Smithson was a businessman, he had made a fortune in armaments. Allan had never liked him. Freddie was getting fat and called him 'old fellow' as though they were real friends. Then there was Peter Robert, a professor of some type at the university, and his wife, Mildred.

Why did university wives look like little girls? he wondered. Were they in awe of their husbands' supposed intellectual capacity? This woman must have been thirty-five yet she had bows in her hair and leather shoes with straps across and a round pleasant face as white and plain as flour. Her husband had a beard. Was that to make him look important?

Why were people invited in twos? He thought of his clerk, Mr Roscommon, whose wife had died just after Allan had left for France in the early months of the war, who had no children and went home alone, and Mrs Semple, his secretary, who had been widowed young.

What did they do in the evenings, people who had no partners, no families? Maybe next time he would suggest to Kaye that they should be invited, at least he would have something in common with them, something to talk about. The only single people invited were Kaye's cousin, Jake, and a woman Kaye had asked to sit next to him who was pretty in a skinny sort of way and liked sport.

There was also Raymond Hedley who had been sent to Ireland in the middle of the war after he married, to do some kind of training. He was the nearest Allan got to conversation that evening, barring Jake, whom Allan considered family.

Raymond's wife was pretty and fashionable and wore a stylish dress. When Allan escaped to the conservatory after the meal she followed him there and kissed him. She had had too much to drink.

He tried to keep this in mind but it was difficult. She was warm and willing in his arms and the novelty appealed to him. He enjoyed it, liked the taste of gin and tonic on her tongue, the juniper smell of her mouth and the feel of her soft body almost naked and warm through the thin material of her evening dress.

With regret he shepherded her back into the drawing room. Kaye looked at him. She was not deceived, he thought admiringly, and he would have to provide some answers later.

In there the talk was of the knight, Angus Ballantine, who had been found dead in his library a week ago.

'His wife did him in, was found with a gun in her hand,' Reggie said, sitting on the arm of the sofa in a way that Kaye would be displeased about, Allan thought, if she were not obliged to be polite. 'Young and gorgeous but very common. Her father is a miner.'

'She allegedly did him in,' Jake said, emerging from the shadows near the window and Allan was struck by how alike Kaye and Jake were, both Nordic looking, except that Jake had inherited his mother's chocolate-brown eyes, whereas Kaye's eyes were icy blue, and she had pale yellow hair. They were more like brother and sister than cousins and neither of them, thankfully, Allan thought, was anything like Reggie, who had taken after his father's side of the family and was dark and sallow.

'Good old Jake,' Reggie said, 'always the legal man.'

Reggie, Allan thought, was jealous of his cousin. Jake was clever and Reggie was not stupid enough not to know it and envied him his ability.

'Stick to the facts, Reggie,' Jake said. 'Nobody knows anything yet.'

'He could have shot himself,' Freddie offered. 'I think I'd shoot myself if I were blind and lame and all my money had gone in death duties.'

'Not if you had a wife as young as that,' Reggie leered.

'He must have been in love,' Freddie's wife said.

'Love, nothing. Lust more like.'

'Why would anybody shoot themselves when they had been married so short a time?' Kaye said with a frown and Allan thought she was right, Kaye had a good logical mind on her.

Reggie laughed.

'Maybe he had made a mistake. Couldn't stand her dreadful accent or lack of manners. Maybe she didn't know which knife and fork to use at dinner.'

Kaye's brow was furrowed. She hated smutty or disparaging talk. Allan was inclined to agree with her. One of the reasons he had married her was because she had a hatred of what she called 'class distinction'.

'One day it won't be like that,' she had said, after a bottle of champagne they had shared shortly after they were married. 'Everybody will have the chance to be educated, everybody will have opportunities, nobody will be poor.'

It was a wonderful idea, Allan thought now and he wondered whether she still believed in it. He escaped once again, this time as far as the library. Were they never going home?

'Had enough?' a voice said behind him and when Allan turned around from the fireplace Jake smiled, pushed his hands into his pockets and came over.

'Saunders has asked me if I'll take the case,' Allan said, staring out into the depths of the bare autumn garden.

'What, the Ballantine woman?'

Jake looked surprised, he thought.

'You think I'm not up to it?'

Jake looked at him and Allan was grateful at the smile Jake gave.

'Of course I think you're up to it. Do you think she did it?'

'I haven't met her yet. What do you think?'

Jake didn't answer immediately but when he did it was with decision.

'She did it,' he said.

'It could have been an accident.'

'Yes, but you know what they say,' and he smiled as they chorused, 'there's no such thing as an accident.'

'He could have been trying to shoot her,' Allan said.

Jake frowned and then he too regarded the garden with more interest than it deserved.

'He was twice as old. She was working class and almost certainly married him for his money—'

'He could have been a perfectly nice man—'

Jake looked cynically at him.

'When was the last time you met a perfectly nice man?' he said. 'We're all bastards. Besides which he was badly injured in the war, blind and almost lame. Why else would a beautiful twenty-year-old marry a middle-aged man but for

75

his apparent wealth and consequence. It must have seemed like a fairy tale to her after a pit row.'

'What are you two doing in here when we have guests?' came Kaye's voice as cool as ice cream from the doorway. 'Are you talking about work?'

'No, we're avoiding the charming young woman you invited for my benefit,' her cousin said.

'You're very rude,' she said, though not convincingly, and Allan thought once again how beautiful she was.

'All she talks about is golf,' Jake said. 'Do you have to have even numbers at your dinner parties? It's archaic.'

She came over and kissed him on the cheek.

'I'm trying to marry you off.'

'Well, don't.'

'Why not? You're a perfectly good man and there's a shortage. Hadn't you heard?'

'One of these days I will wring your neck,' Jake said but he kissed her too.

When the evening was over and Kaye had seen the last people to the door she came back into the drawing room where Allan had lingered and said, 'If you must have a little trollop at least choose one who hasn't slept with half the county.'

'I didn't—'

'Oh, don't deny it, please.'

'She was drunk, that was all.' Allan had rehearsed what he was going to say. Unfortunately he could not resist, 'And don't tell me that it matters to you.'

'Our respectability matters to me. I would rather not hear your name bandied about through gossip and don't say that nobody noticed, everybody did. She spent the entire evening slavering over you. Did you have to take her out there? It looked so obvious.'

Allan was about to argue and then didn't. He said nothing and was just thinking that he had enough control over himself to go to bed when his wife said, 'Are you going to take the Ballantine case?'

'Do you think I should?'

Kaye looked straight at him.

76

'You've been home for months and so far you've done nothing. I would be glad of any case you took.'

'Well,' he said, 'perhaps I will,' and then he went to bed.

Jake had arrived back from France to find that Mrs Coulthard was still living in his house and to his surprise his father had given her a job in the chambers which Jake and his father owned in Old Elvet.

'It's a very good arrangement,' his father said, 'I pay her sufficient for her to have help with the child and food and since she's living in your house she pays no rent and it works all round, cheap for her and . . . I have to say I find her very competent.'

'And what did my mother think about it?'

'It was nothing to do with your mother,' his father said, a trifle defensively, which meant that his mother had obviously made a fuss about it and his father had dug his heels in as he was wont to do when crossed. His mother had never learned. And then his father hesitated and said, 'She's a very nice young woman for all her appearance and nobody else would employ her. What was I meant to do?'

'I'm sorry I put you into that position.'

'I'm sorry too,' his father said gruffly.

His mother had more to say on the subject.

'It isn't quite nice to have a young woman like that living in your house. It's far too big for her. If you want to have tenants there you should have someone who will pay rent properly. Mrs Coulthard can't need more than a room or two for herself and a small child. And I don't think your father should have taken her on at your chambers. Whatever will people think of us, employing women like that?'

Jake wanted to ask, 'Women like what?' but he didn't have time to argue and in any case there was no point in arguing with his mother, she didn't listen. She had obviously thought he had got over losing Madeline and was, rather like Kaye had assumed, ready to get married again. She kept inviting various young women to dinner. Jake stayed at his chambers, having been asked to take on the case and agreed to do so.

77

His father said, 'She can hardly hope to marry again, after all. She'll have to do something with her life. Offered to move out when she heard you were coming home but I didn't think you wanted to go there and live.'

'Quite right,' Jake said, 'I didn't.'

He knew what his father meant about Lilian Coulthard marrying again. She was coloured and it mattered, most especially to people of his father's generation, but at least his father had helped her.

Jake got a shock when he went to see Lilian, as he did as soon as he got back, before they met at work. It was so almost Madeline in so many ways. He knew that he had contrived in his head to make her almost Madeline and that in fact she was nothing like but she was in his house with a baby and he was desperate to see his wife. He hadn't realized he would become more and more lonely as time went on, he had thought it would get better.

Lilian was even prettier than she had been, under his father's capable care and even better, or worse, depending on how you looked at it, she was so aware of everything they had done for her, so grateful, so unwilling to assume anything.

Jake wished in a way that she had been brash and greedy and he would have felt no compunction whatsoever about putting her down on the sofa in the sitting room and having her in the uncomplicated way that his body screamed for. But he couldn't.

The savage in him wanted to but the gentleman wouldn't let him. And he could have laughed at himself for this supposed sophistication. Where had it come from when he had come back from almost five years of basic living?

In a way it was out of respect to Madeline that he did not touch Lilian Coulthard but mostly it was because the woman who was living in his house obviously expected that he would take advantage of the situation and he had seen the fear and expectation in her eyes and he wanted to maintain the illusion that he was nice for as long as possible.

He saw her at work and they maintained a politeness but he went to the house very little and always in the middle of the day on Saturdays. He did not expect invitations to eat or to stay for more than a very short time and she had already said to him that she was finding somewhere more suited to her means to live, this house was too big and that she would move out should Jake wish to move back in, he had only to say so.

In his better moments, while he was sitting in his chambers on Sunday afternoons, which he did more and more just to get away from his parents, he would think of her there in the pale winter afternoons with the baby by the fire and he thought, in a stupid sense, that Madeline was watching over her, that Madeline wanted her to be there, was glad. It was just his own ridiculous sentimental self, Jake thought but he didn't care. It was the only thing which comforted him.

Eleven

It was Sunday. On Sundays Allan and Kaye always went to Jake's parents for a big meal in South Street in the middle of the city. The house was huge and terraced and sat right across the river from the cathedral and castle and had the most wonderful views.

Allan had never learned to appreciate Sunday dinner. Even when he had been away she had come here every week to her aunt and uncle and Reggie and a tradition so long established could not be broken for what they would think of as a whim.

Jake was missing that day and Reggie was still in bed, no doubt sleeping off the hangover from the day before. His aunt and uncle indulged him because he had taken it so badly when his parents died when he was very young. Allan's parents had died when he was small too but nobody had indulged him.

He had been sent off to boarding school and then to spend his holidays in London with distant relatives. It had been hideous. His father's cousins had not wanted him. They were a childless couple with a social life and thought they had done their duty when they had fed him and told him he must go to bed. Perhaps that was what he resented so much about Reggie, that somebody had loved him sufficiently to take him in and look after him properly rather than seeing him as a nuisance to be ignored until he grew up and was fit for civilized company.

The few childhood memories Allan had of Jake's parents was of Jake's mother putting him on a train to take him away to school after his mother had died. The look of relief on her face was something he had not forgotten. She had not kissed him or touched him at all, she just put him on the train.

80

Allan was thinking about Erin Ballantine and what she must be like. He had spent a lot of time trying to decide whether to take the case and now—

'My aunt says the meal is ready,' Kaye said, coming into the small sitting room where he stood alone, gazing into the log fire.

It was always the same, a small sherry before the meal – he had made an excuse and left the drawing room just as this happened, somehow he couldn't bear it – and then they would have water with the meal, a huge roast, it was pork with crackling, apple sauce, thick gravy, tureens full of Brussels sprouts, carrots and cabbage, Yorkshire puddings, golden and round.

When he had been in France he had longed for this. Now he didn't want it but he went into the dining room with her and tried to regard the enormous meal with some enthusiasm. After he had failed to make any impression on the food which sat mountainous on his plate her aunt said, 'You're not eating anything, Allan.'

'I'm not very hungry.'

She looked at her husband and then at Kaye and when neither of them spoke she said, 'We think you should see a doctor.'

It was a minute or so before Allan realized, firstly that she was speaking to him and secondly that she was serious. He stared at her.

'What do you mean?'

'You don't eat. You spend hours staring at nothing. You never have anything to say and Kaye says you sleepwalk.'

Allan looked at his wife but she wasn't looking at him.

'A lot of men have come back from this war badly damaged,' her aunt said.

Badly damaged, Allan thought, it made him sound like a mishandled parcel.

'We're all very worried about you. We don't think you should have taken this Ballantine case. We think it may well be too much for you to manage.'

'I am not damaged, badly or otherwise,' Allan said, looking at Jake's father for support and seeing nothing, and it provided him with an excuse to leave the huge plateful of food which had defeated his appetite.

He went outside. It was almost dark, one of those bleak, short, cold, damp days before Christmas. After a few moments he heard footsteps behind him on the garden path and then his wife's voice.

'Do come inside, Allan, you'll catch your death out here.'

She stood just behind him on the path. She wouldn't want to get her elegant shoes wet so she didn't follow him even when he started off across the sopping lawns away from her.

She shouted his name twice and when Allan increased his speed of step she ran after him, only stopping short when he turned around.

'How did you know I was sleepwalking?' he demanded. 'What did I do, try to get into bed with you?'

Tears drenched Kaye's beautiful eyes.

'I want my husband back,' she said. 'You must go to the doctor, Allan, I don't recognize you. I was so very much in love with you. Now you don't speak for days and days and I don't know what you're thinking any more. We used to know one another so well, we used to be so happy.' She stopped there and began to cry.

'Go back inside,' Allan said. 'I'm not going to any doctor, Kaye, and you can tell your aunt and uncle that if I hear any more about this I'll stop at home on Sundays and that way I won't have to face any more mounds of bloody green vegetables,' and Allan smiled at his own witticism and set off through the trees so fast that a squirrel fled over the long leaf-strewn grass and ran up a Chinese ivy tree, the black berries hung like small bunches of grapes.

He had loved this place when he was a little boy, it was so neat, so orderly, the young trees with little square fences around them for protection, the bigger ones strongly established. They were safe here. He had never been safe. He had not been taken in like Reggie and Kaye. Nobody had wanted him and since there had been no family connection it had not occurred to the Armstrong family to provide a home for him even after his godmother died. He had, he thought,

82

shocked, never forgiven them for it, had perhaps even married Kaye hoping to gain her extended family.

As the light began to go the silence grew around him, coming down like a cloak with fog in the afternoon and he could hear the bells from the cathedral, calling people in toward evensong.

He had loved that too at one time, the way that only the front of the cathedral was lit, the little boys singing, the dusk gathering outside. He had liked the comfort there. Now he couldn't go into the cathedral and feel anything but hatred for God but he did remember coming out into the cold darkness, returning home, see the cream lights from the drawing room where his mother would be toasting crumpets by the fire, pouring tea from the big silver teapot.

The house which had belonged to his mother's family in North End had been his home. It had been sold after his mother died and it was a huge loss to him though for practicality's sake he could hardly have lived in two houses.

When his education had been complete he came home to claim Hedleyhope House but he could not help sometimes going past the house in North End and watching through the windows and remembering being there with his mother after his father had died and how she had cried and how they had clung together in the early years when he was very small. It was somebody else's home now. He was shut out forever.

And all those men who had died in the mud in France where it never seemed to stop raining would not do such a thing again, would not come home to their families and comfort and warmth and toasted crumpets and tea and strawberry jam by the fire on winter afternoons and he realized then that in a way he would never come back either. The innocence, the hope, the idea of a future, it was all gone.

Twelve

The coroner's court decided that there was a case to answer and Allan drove to Heath Houses to meet Erin Ballantine. He was preceded down the street by a volley of urchins, ragged, skinny and enthusiastic. Since he had come back from France he had thought himself a wretched unlucky man but here amidst the pit rows and the crowd of dirty children's faces he was ashamed. He thought of Laurie doing his lessons and of how much his parents cared for him. He stopped the Morris Cowley and got out. The children hung back. Only one of them said wistfully, 'Nice car, mister.'

Allan smiled briefly and went up to the front door of number nine and banged on it. After what seemed like a long interval it was opened by a small fat woman in a wrapover pinafore. When he explained his business she blushed, pulled off her pinny and ushered him inside.

'Eh, Mr Jamieson, if I'd known it was you. Come in and I'll get our Erin.'

She took him into a sitting room, small, dark, with net curtains across the window for privacy. Allan wondered what it was like living so closely with one's neighbours. No fire burned there, the empty grate looked hollow and dead in the cold of the winter's day. Allan could see his breath.

He turned around when he heard a noise behind him and then stared. The most beautiful girl in the whole world stood in the doorway. She had eyes the colour of almonds, skin like icing sugar, a mouth that must have made every man who saw her want to kiss her, hair like cinnamon. She was tall, slender. This was Erin Ballantine. No wonder Sir Angus had wanted her.

'Lady Ballantine?'

She was staring too as though she recognized him though he was certain they had not met before.

'I never got used to it,' she said and he thought her simplicity was charming.

'I'm Allan Jamieson.'

'Yes. Yes, I know.' She paused there and then seemed to recollect why he was there. 'Everybody knows your family. Your dad was so well thought of, my dad says, he always championed people who had nothing. I'm sorry you had to come here. I can't stay in that place. Diana – that's Angus's sister – she doesn't want me there.'

Allan tried to get used to the perfection of her so that he could talk normally but it wasn't easy.

'You need somebody with experience and . . . somebody very competent to defend you.'

'I was told you were the best.'

Allan looked down at his hat. It was a good thing he had not relinquished it because his hands shook. They needed something to hold.

'It was a long time ago,' he said.

'But you – you defend people like me.'

Allan could feel his face burn under her gaze. He thought back to the person he had been before the war, so arrogant, so sure of himself, taking on the courts and beating them and trying to help the people who had so little. Kaye had fallen in love with that brash, clever person. And, he could not help adding silently, out of love with the person he was now.

'Lady Ballantine—'

'You can call me Erin. After all, we'll be seeing a lot of each other, won't we?'

'You need somebody better than me.'

'There is nobody better than you, my dad says you've defended lots of people and got them off. He said it's a – a tradition in your family. Your dad started it and you carried it on.'

It made Allan so pleased that the people around Durham thought of his father that way but he knew in a way that Jake's parents were right and he wasn't up to this.

85

'I haven't . . . the war . . .'

'Mr Jamieson, if you won't help me I'm lost. They'll – they'll hang me. They think I killed Angus. The police think so.'

'I could find you somebody else. There are any number of good barristers—'

'I don't want anybody else. I want you.'

They were, in another sense, the words he had so much wished his wife to say.

At that moment her mother appeared with a tray, tea and a full round fruit cake on a lace cloth and she had obviously tidied her hair and changed her dress and she had that look on her face, the look that could not believe things had gone so badly. The look of unwarranted disaster.

That was when Allan remembered. The brash young lawyer he had been was a champion to people like these. They loved that about him. They admired that he tried to bring them justice. He must pretend to be that man still, for all their sakes.

'Why, Mrs Marsden, what a wonderful cake,' he said and she beamed.

Erin had thought Allan Jamieson would be like Felix Saunders. Mr Saunders was middle-aged, old enough to have a wife and three children. He was a kind man and quite clever she thought, smiling on her and telling her that everything would be all right while the worry went on in his eyes. She wished she could not see it.

He stood up for her in court and at the inquest and it was through him that she got to go home. She had had the awful feeling she would be sitting in some cold damp room for the next however many weeks it took before they brought her to trial and she didn't know how she was going to bear that. She was so grateful to Mr Saunders for helping her. She said to him, 'Will you be there at the trial?'

'No, we need a barrister for that,' and he explained to her what would happen in as little detail as possible so that he did not frighten her but she was frightened. Also she had grown used to him and had learned to trust him, she did not want to deal with another man.

Mr Saunders wrote her a letter several days after she got home, telling her that he had prevailed upon Allan Jamieson to come and see her. There was nothing fixed but they would talk and it would be decided whether he was the right person to represent her. Her dad read the letter and said, 'Oh yes, he's a grand lad. His dad was the best lawyer in the county, everybody said so. He could get you off anything and Allan had a good reputation for all he's so young, before the war.'

When she saw Allan Jamieson for the first time she was surprised that he was so young. Barristers were highly educated men but even so he did not seem middle-aged like Mr Saunders and he certainly didn't look like he had a wife and children.

He was big, that was the first thing, and she hadn't thought of that. Mr Saunders was short like her dad. Mr Jamieson was not big like Angus had been. There was nothing ungainly about him, he was tall and had black hair and pale skin, Scottish-looking almost, definitely a border man. He had a disconcerting way of shooting you very straight looks from dark grey eyes as though he knew everything about you the moment he set eyes on you.

He looked like the sort of man that anybody could hide against and that was what she liked best about him. Allan Jamieson was capable of putting himself like a barrier between her and the rest of the world. Also he had a lovely voice, she thought, soft but decisive. Her mother blushed when he complimented her on the cake and she thought, yes, women would fancy him. She didn't. She had had two experiences of men lately and they could cost her her life.

She saw him to the door and down the lane where his car stood.

'When will you decide whether you'll help me?' and she turned and looked into his eyes and then she knew what she had wanted from a man. He said, 'I've already decided. I'll take on the case and I'll look after you but you have to promise me two things.'

'Anything.'

'Firstly that you won't lie to me.'

'I won't.'

'And secondly that you'll trust me completely no matter how bad things seem to get.'

'I'll do that.'

'All right, then.' He smiled at her just a little. 'Don't worry,' he said, 'everything's going to be fine.'

Erin wished she could have somehow been able to keep Allan Jamieson and that slight smile and him saying, 'Everything's going to be fine.'

When she lay in bed at night as the days went by before the trial she brought the memory back of standing outside the house in Lilac Street with him and knowing that what every woman wanted from every man was to be looked after like he was going to look after her. She tried not to think about Kelvin, they could not help one another now.

Allan went to see Jake. He needed support.

'It's a cast-iron case, Allan,' Jake said. 'We have the gun. She was found with it in her hand.'

'By his sister. She could have been lying.'

Jake looked pityingly at him.

'He could have killed himself deliberately,' Allan said.

'His brains would be all over the floor. You're deluding yourself. The best you can hope for is that there was a quarrel and a struggle and I don't think you'll get away with that. The man was blind. How could he hope to shoot anybody even himself cleanly and as for her, to a jury she's a common little workman's daughter. She married him for greed and then couldn't stand the life because he was a disabled man. I have to admit, though, I think there's something missing.'

Jake sat back in his chair and Allan was reminded of what life had been like before the war. They had spent so many evenings like this, drinking whisky over the fire in Jake's chambers or his own, talking about the various cases they were dealing with.

Jake's chambers were in Old Elvet. The rooms at this side looked across the river. At one time Allan had liked the view. Now he didn't. Rivers and cathedrals, they went on and on. People didn't. Allan could see the houses across the river from there, one of them was the house where Jake and Madeline had lived together.

The whisky glasses were big and when Jake got up and refilled them the amount he put in them matched. Allan took a slug and closed his eyes as it went down his throat. Perhaps whisky was all there was left.

'I don't think she did it,' Allan said.

'Oh yes?' Jake's eyes gleamed with amusement. 'Now that you've met her?'

'Have you?'

'I like conversation, wit, sophistication, not those kind of superior shop-girl looks.'

Allan couldn't help laughing. Madeline had been clever, witty. He ached just to think of her. She lit the rooms she walked into with her smile and her laughter.

'Perhaps Erin Ballantine hasn't had the chance yet. She seemed bright to me.'

'Anybody would look bright to you,' Jake said, with the deprecating look of a good friend.

Allan was flattered. It was the first time Jake had insulted him in months. Jake looked closely at him.

'You all right?'

'Your mother and father have been talking to you about me,' Allan guessed.

'You are awfully skinny and . . .'

'And?' They had not come on so very far, Allan reflected, as he nodded and did not tell Jake any truths. Jake didn't answer. So Allan returned to the subject.

'What did you mean, something missing?'

Jake frowned.

'I don't know. I can understand that she might kill him if he treated her badly, but is there evidence of it?'

'We had an argument,' Erin had said. 'He took the gun out of the drawer. I thought he was going to try and kill me. We struggled and it went off.'

'But when his sister came into the room you had the gun in your hand.'

'I know.'

89

'So tell me exactly what happened.'

'The gun went off and he was lying on the floor and then I . . . I picked it up.'

'Why did you pick it up?'

'I can't remember. I can't remember doing it.'

'Why were you arguing?'

'About the house. Angus was determined to sell it and had found a buyer for it. I was very much against it.' Enough to kill to prevent him? Allan wondered. And that wasn't the truth, he thought.

'It wasn't himself he was trying to kill?'

She looked confused. Allan understood completely why people killed themselves. The world they had all come back to seemed so futile and Sir Angus had had a young wife and yet was middle-aged, blind, couldn't walk far. Perhaps he couldn't perform in bed. Allan hadn't asked that.

He knew that Sir Angus was in debt without likelihood of being able to hold on to the house which his ancestors had built and which undoubtedly he loved very much. Perhaps his marriage to a young and beautiful woman had been the last straw. Perhaps he had thought to kill them both and thus solve all their problems.

And he could understand how a man like that would not keep her happy or satisfied. He had met the sister. He had gone to the house by the river and walked up the path and looked long and hard at it and wondered whether a love for such a house and the fear of losing it might make a woman like Erin Ballantine kill. Diana Ballantine was convinced that her sister-in-law had killed him.

'I walked in and she was standing over him. They had been unhappy most of the time of their marriage.' She put her hands to her throat as though she didn't want to say the next bit and then took them away.

'He should never have married her. She thought she was escaping the awful life she led in a pit cottage and he thought he was escaping the loneliness of his blindness and it didn't work. I could see from the beginning that it wouldn't. I think she thought he had money though where she got that idea

90

from I don't know. I think she was disappointed, she seemed to think we lived a high life.'

Diana smiled slightly. 'All our friends deserted us when Angus was so badly hurt. He had been going to get married.'

'And you?'

'I didn't expect to marry.'

Her expectations had been correct, Allan thought, she was too upper middle-class for any man to consider, thin, plain, penniless.

He had also talked to Erin Ballantine at length, in her mother's front room, and she had tried to imply at one point that Sir Angus had taken the gun from the drawer to kill himself.

'I made his life worse. He had been so comfortable, so resigned, but after we were married he wished to be . . . to be able to see me, to be able to run, for us to do the things together that he had wished we could because I was so young.'

Marriage to her would have been enough for some men, Allan thought, but there was more to it. She was not telling him the truth. Please God she hadn't done it. If she was lying to him . . .

'Was it a good marriage?'

She blushed.

'I don't know. I have little to compare it with except my parents and it seems to me that they ask so little of one another. My father works and goes to the pub once a week with his friends. My mother keeps house and seems content cleaning and cooking and looking after us and then sitting over the fire with her knitting. They have so little, want so little.'

'And you wanted more?'

'You make it sound wrong.'

'I didn't mean to. I'm just trying to understand what happened here.'

'I didn't kill him, Mr Jamieson, really I didn't.'

'I didn't think you did.'

She looked relieved and then her mouth quivered.

'You don't mean that. You don't have to believe me to defend me, do you?'

91

'No, but it helps. I don't think you're capable of killing anyone.'

Now, sitting in Jake's chambers, Allan doubted himself for perhaps the thousandth time and it occurred to him that anybody but Jake would be glad to take on a case which had a weak defence, a weak barrister. Jake was watching him.

'Do you think I'm ill, like your parents do?' Allan said.

'No. I think you should take the case on. Think of all the fun we'll have fighting over it in court and sitting here of an evening. It'll be like old times. Come on, Allan, you can do it.'

'She's not guilty,' Allan said, 'and I'm going to beat you to the ground.'

Jake laughed. Allan loved to hear it. Almost like old times except that Jake was going home to bed alone and so was he. What would Jake have thought if Allan had told him that Kaye would not let him past the bedroom door and he was desperate with want, except that he wasn't, that was the awful part somehow.

In some ways he wanted never to care for anyone again so that when people died he could mourn briefly and get over it, move on and be happy. Maybe that was what Kaye had seen in him, that increasing need to keep away from other people and that was why she didn't want him.

He could not tell her that he had wept when a horse drowned in mud, had not cried over his men, many of whom had died so bravely. In some ways he had wanted never to hear a Durham accent again, all those pitmen turned soldier, but when he met Erin Ballantine everything was different.

He wanted to go on listening to her, to hear the rhythm of her words in his sleep, it was somehow the homecoming he had lacked. This was a woman he could have an affair with, not Raymond's silly wife. He wished he could have sat over the fire with her forever in her mother's front room.

Thirteen

Christmas. There were trees covered in white candles in the cathedral. Allan knew because Kaye had made him go to a carol service. He couldn't even remember the words and stood there, watching the way that the candles flickered and listening to the choir and the mighty organ. What did they hope to achieve, he wondered?

He was only glad when they could leave. Kaye put her hand through his arm and smiled at him and Laurie walked on his other side and he should have felt happy because he was there.

Laurie had come home very quiet. Allan longed to ask him if he would like not to go back but he couldn't. What would Laurie do if he hated school? You couldn't fail at nine, it was asking too much. By now if he was liking it he would not come home so pale and thin and it worried Allan into the far reaches of the night.

Christmas Day dawned and for once Allan had got it right. Laurie's eyes lit when he saw the train set and he said, 'Can we set it up right now?'

Allan said, 'Right now.'

Laurie said, 'Topping!'

And Kaye laughed at their pleasure and went off to the kitchen to see about food.

It was a wonderful day. Jake and his parents and Reggie came for dinner and they all played with the train set and there were lots of presents. It even snowed. The trains went round and round and the men were fascinated and Laurie was so proud. There was a green engine and a blue one and a red one and a black coal train and lots of trucks and carriages.

Allan wished he could hang on to the day, make it last,

put it into a glass case like men did with animals they had killed – how could they do it? – killing. It never stopped.

The day ended and even when it did he went over and over it in his mind like a secret treasure, committing each part to memory, the dusk in mid-afternoon when the candles on the Christmas tree were bright and there was food and wine on the table and then dusk and finally night. He would have given anything to hold it back. When Laurie went to bed he put both arms around Allan's neck and said, 'Thank you, Dad, I had a wizard day.'

'I'm so glad,' Allan said. 'I had a wizard day too.'

The day before Laurie was due to go back to school he stood amidst the open trunk and the organized mess of packing on the bed and Allan came to the doorway and knocked softly until the boy turned around.

'Are you all right?' Allan said.

'Yes, of course.'

While Allan had been away Laurie had obviously been told amongst all the other lies that boys didn't cry and was swallowing as many tears as he could manage while scrubbing at the moisture left on his face, including his nose with a now less than clean sleeve.

He was a solitary child, he didn't seem to have many friends, whereas Allan remembered his early boyhood, streams and rocks and cricket bats and cold afternoons hiding in the long grass beside the railway while others searched for him in game.

Every time he suggested to Kaye that Laurie should play with another child she brushed it aside if the child was not socially of their circle but he could see by now that mostly Laurie didn't want other children, he was happy sitting over the fire with a book and it was unfair to blame Kaye.

Allan, standing there and not being asked into the room, was disabused of the idea that Christmas had brought them closer and horrified at how much love he felt for the small skinny person in front of him and vowed he would never offer up his life again for anyone else.

'You don't have to go.'

Laurie looked at him in astonishment.

'You think I want to stay here, the way that things are?'

Allan was astonished. Firstly at the accusing way his son looked at him, secondly that Laurie was mature enough to realize there was something wrong between his parents and thirdly that he would have enough nerve to say such things to his father.

'What do you mean?'

'You and . . . you and Mother. You came back and spoiled everything.'

Allan stared at his child, while Laurie stared back, suddenly rigid and white, and that was the first time that Allan realized his child was afraid of him, without reason, he thought, and worse still it became obvious in those moments that Laurie disliked, perhaps even hated, him. Regardless of fear Laurie stumbled on and the tears ran unchecked down his small, pale face. He was almost shouting.

'We were fine until you came home. You upset her all the time. How can you do that? You're . . . you're . . . I'm glad to go back to school rather than stay here with you,' and he ran from the room.

The following day Laurie went. Allan made himself stay in chambers. He thought of the decanter of port which Mr Roscommon kept in the cupboard in the main office and he went through and there it was, almost full.

He took the decanter and a glass – not a port glass, a proper wine glass – into his office and sat with his feet up on the window ledge and watched the evening darken across the cathedral and he wondered at the kind of society where men lived impossibly and died worse and built such elegant useless buildings.

He trudged home through thick snow and Kaye came into the hall, her step quick.

'I was getting worried about you.'

'There was no need.'

'I kept the dinner long past the usual time.'

'You shouldn't have bothered. How was Laurie's school?' She and her aunt and uncle had taken him back.

'The same as it was when it was your school, I imagine.'

95

'God, I hope not,' he said and went through into the sitting room.

She followed him there.

'Have you been drinking?'

He wanted to laugh at the disapproval in her voice. He wasn't to have sex. He wasn't to have alcohol. What in hell was he to have? When he didn't answer immediately she said, 'Did you go to the pub with friends?' as though he should have let her know. Somehow this was acceptable. He wondered which friends she thought these were. His friends were buried in France, the men of the Durham Light Infantry, all those men who had made his life bearable.

He sat gazing at the single decanter which sat on a small table in the corner as though they were ashamed of it.

'Don't we have anything to drink but bloody sherry?'

'Did you have any lunch?'

'How long have you been my mother, Kaye?'

'Since you started behaving like a small child.'

'You really don't like me much any more, do you?' Allan said, considering her carefully as he would not have done sober.

'No, not much.'

She looked clearly at him from the exquisite blue eyes that had been one of the physical things he had liked at the beginning. She had been wearing a blue silk dress that matched them and he had liked how neat and slight and small she was. What a stupid reason for asking a girl to dance. The dress had been decorated with tiny pearls and she had worn silver evening gloves.

'You used to be a gentleman,' she said. 'Now you're just . . .' She stopped and moved back slightly as though he had moved towards her, which he hadn't. 'I'm sorry, I don't mean to be rude. You shouldn't annoy me. I know you've been through a great deal and that it's crass to say you've changed. We've all changed, even those of us whom you seem to think are ignorant of the horrors of war. I know it was awful for you. It wasn't much fun being here without you for more than four years, pretending to be . . . to be jolly when you came home after . . . after . . .'

'After you had fallen out of love with me?'

'Exactly,' she said, eyes bright.

'If there's somebody else—'

'Why do men always think that? Are you so conceited that you couldn't imagine I would learn to dislike you, that there had to be another man? You can't think what it was like, people coming to me and telling me how wonderful it was that you were mentioned in dispatches, that you were a war hero. How lovely for me that my husband won the Victoria Cross, that he risked his life to save other men, how proud I must be of him.' She stopped there. Then she said, 'I'm sorry, that wasn't what I meant. Of course I was proud of you for doing such a thing.'

'No, no,' Allan said. 'It would be simplistic indeed to explain away one's regard in medals. Do you want me to leave?'

'Certainly not. We have Laurie to think about and you have your brilliant career.'

Her voice was sweetly sour and he understood. Before the war his reputation had been something else she could be proud of. Now he seemed to do nothing but stare out across Palace Green all day. 'There is some whisky in the dining-room cabinet. Shall I get it?' she said.

'Yes, please.'

At that moment if Allan had not loved his house so much or if he had had anywhere else to go he would have gone but there was nobody and nothing.

'Are we supposed to go on permanently with this charade?' he said when she came back.

'I'm sure hundreds of people do likewise,' Kaye said and she presented the whisky to him and went to bed.

It was unfortunate that he could hear her crying as she tried to make a dignified exit.

Allan had made Erin Ballantine go back to the house where her husband had died. He had wanted to see her reaction. When he suggested it she went pale and her mother protested faintly – they were in the front room at the house in Lilac Street at the time.

'I don't want her to have to go back to that house, Mr Jamieson, not after what happened.'

'Diana is staying with friends,' Allan said.

'She doesn't have any friends,' Erin said.

'Well, she's found some from somewhere and is staying in Jesmond in Newcastle at the moment. I think it's important that we go there together and that you talk me through what happened there. You needn't worry, Mrs Marsden, I'll look after her.'

When Allan had seen the house for the first time he understood at least in part why she had married Angus Ballantine. It appealed to him as his own house did. It was beautiful. It rose up from the riverbank in a long meadow and the front part sat on high ground with gardens running into one another as though the whole thing was some elaborate game. His second impression reinforced the first thoughts. It was a wonderful house.

To one side was the earliest bit, the gloomiest part, and Allan could imagine someone dying here, especially in the gloomy chamber which she said had been their bedroom with its huge empty fireplace and dark corners. It was the least comfortable bedroom he had ever seen.

The wind whistled in through the windows, the draught howled under the door. The bed was four-poster and looked very old and the mattress . . . he could see how it sagged, and shuddered to think how many people might have given birth, had sex and died on the damned thing.

He could never have slept on it. It was thin, ragged and looked lumpy. The furniture in that room was Jacobean, ugly, some of it carved with eagles with huge beaks. He could well imagine someone dying here.

She led him slowly down the stairs, which were meant to be haunted, he was not surprised, through the light, airy hall and into the library where Sir Angus had died. Allan found it was a wonderful room, light with small-paned Georgian windows and friendly looking bookcases. It looked out across the sloping front gardens towards the city and he could see the towers of the cathedral, sparkling in the morning winter sunshine.

Erin showed him inside but did not go in at first, she hovered in the doorway and then as Allan said, 'Was this where it happened?' she said, 'Yes.' Her voice was low and she began to look around her at the shadows behind the curtains and the gloom where the sun did not reach.

'Tell me about it.'

'I said, it was just a quarrel.'

'Over the house?'

'Yes.'

'Are you certain that's all?'

She looked at him.

'Quite certain.'

'It seems a small matter to quarrel so violently about.'

'It wasn't violently, at least not at first.'

'Come in. Come on, come inside. It's all right, I'm here.'

She did but slowly, carefully.

'He had sold the house and I loved it so much, you see. I don't love it any more. It was . . .'

'It was what?'

'Nothing.'

'Erin, you have to trust me.'

It was the first time he had called her by her first name though she had long since invited him to do so.

'I loved the house so much,' she said softly. 'I didn't want to live without it. I'd never had a nice house before.' She looked at him. 'You've seen how my parents live, no space, no view, no comforts, going on at somebody else's pace for somebody else's benefit.

'My father has worked down that pit all his life and for what? The coal owners are rich. All we ever did was get by. My parents don't mind because they love one another but I wanted a house of my own and Broke Hall was perfect, is perfect. I didn't want to lose it and he sold it without even consulting me.

'He and Diana, they always did things without telling me as though I wasn't part of the family. I was never included, like I was a child, or stupid, or unimportant. I just went to work and tipped up my pay. In some ways it was as bad as being at home.' She smiled slightly. 'In some ways it was worse.'

'What ways?' Allan asked softly.

She didn't answer that. After he had given her enough time he said, 'What happened? Talk me through it.'

'He became very angry and took this little silver pistol out of the desk drawer there. I'd never seen it before. Being blind he never touched things like that. Diana did the only shooting in the family and that was just rabbits and . . . things for the pot. There was a shotgun for that over the mantelpiece in the study.'

'And then?'

'I thought he was going to shoot me or himself, I wasn't sure which, and I tried to stop him and . . . and we over-balanced and the gun went off. It was an accident, Mr Jamieson, you have to believe me.'

'I do.'

'I've never seen a gun before other than the shotguns you see people killing pigeons and rabbits with. Do you know what the worst thing is?'

Allan waited.

'The house is mine and even if I came through this and won and everything was all right I could never live here now, not after what happened, not after Angus died because we quarrelled.'

And she must never be allowed to say anything like that in court, Allan decided. He would coach her. She had picked the gun up after the man had deliberately or otherwise killed himself. She would hang if there was any dispute about it. She was, he thought, slightly unhinged, but who wouldn't be after what had occurred?

'Diana hates me. She thinks I did it. How could she think so? I loved them both very much. I wanted them to treat me like an equal and in some ways I was jealous of how close they were. I had a brother and he died in France. We were close too. I miss that.'

'I suppose for her it was an easier option than thinking that her beloved brother might be violent either towards you or himself.'

'He went through a war. Doesn't that make men violent?'

It certainly made the lack of violence seem strange when

100

you came home and attempted to take up the reins of what was apparently a civilized society, the society which had given up all those men to die.

'And men naturally are, aren't they?' she said.

Allan thought of all the training they went through to make them so and of one of his men, who was twenty, who had got it wrong and killed his best friend by mistake and thereafter shot himself because he couldn't live with it.

Erin tried to leave the room at that point. Allan got hold of her, gently but by both arms.

'Tell me what happened after that.'

She didn't look at him but at the floor.

'The gun went off. It was awful. It was so awful and I had the feeling that he was not hurt and that he would try to shoot me and . . .' She stopped there.

'The gun went off in Sir Angus's hands,' Allan said.

'He – he fell and hit his head and the gun was lying further over and . . .' She raised her eyes. 'I picked it up but I wasn't going to shoot him, Mr Jamieson, I wasn't. I just wanted to stop him. I was so afraid that he wasn't dead and that he would try to kill me.'

If she ever got into the witness box Jake would tear her apart, Allan thought, but that must be the official version, no matter what had really happened. She wrenched free. He let her go. He could hear the sound of her sobbing as she ran from the room and out towards the front door.

They had, or she had, Kaye corrected herself, planned a dinner party for Saturday of that week but Allan didn't come back, as she had half thought he would not. She didn't even look up as Mary cleared the debris from the dining room. The meal had been tasteless and Kaye blamed herself.

The cook, Mrs Mackenzie, produced good meals, not particularly inspiring. She was a traditional Scottish cook. She was good at pastry, shortbread. The puddings were always the best of it but Kaye could barely remember what the pudding had been. Also the servants were all Allan's choice and she always felt as though they preferred him to her.

Not that any of them was disrespectful but she had the

feeling that if any of them had thought anything she wanted was not what Allan would have approved they would have been very slow carrying out her orders and it made her feel vulnerable. She had had to hold herself together somehow, expecting at any moment that Allan would come home.

She felt humiliated, unwanted. Indeed, she had gone into the kitchen, having sent Mrs Mackenzie off to put her feet up, fetched the pudding herself and Nell, one of her friends, followed her in there and said in a kind of whisper, 'Where is Allan, Kaye? Is everything all right?'

Kaye could feel how tight her face was. She had done a lot of weeping lately. She hoped it didn't show. She had never thought her marriage would unravel like a piece of bad knitting. Somehow she had clung to the idea that after Allan came home for good things would get better. It was as though it was going downhill and she was trying to run after it and retrieve it and it would not be retrieved. She could not understand what was happening. The harder she tried to make a home and a social life for them the worse it got.

'Yes, of course. Just working late in chambers. Sometimes he cannot get away. Most unfortunate. People come in as he's leaving in the evenings very often. He has taken on the Ballantine case and there is a great deal to do.'

'He's changed a lot since the war,' Nell said and the relief of knowing that somebody else had recognized this made Kaye utter, 'He has, hasn't he?'

'He used to care about things like books and art. Now he doesn't seem to care for anything,' Nell said and when her guests had gone this was what Kaye remembered. The words went round and round in her head.

It was very late indeed when he came home. She had lain awake, listening to the wind as it left Pelaw Woods and made its way back towards the town and she could hear it upon the river. Sometimes she even thought she could hear it whistling amongst the cathedral towers and across Palace Green, moaning its way through the narrow cobbled streets which made up the small city.

She heard him climb the stairs but he wouldn't come into

102

her room. She had never thought they would have separate rooms. She had been so eager to marry him, so much in love. He would not come back without being invited and she did not know how to take him into her arms any more.

The house descended into silence after he shut his door.

At breakfast the following morning she could not resist saying to him, 'Did you forget that people were invited to dinner?'

Allan looked blankly at her and then he said, 'Doesn't that seem a bit pointless to you?'

'I'm trying to keep up a front.'

Allan laughed. Kaye didn't think any of it was funny. Later that day her aunt and uncle came over and her aunt said, 'Would you like to come and stay with us for a while?'

Her uncle had made an excuse and gone out into the garden and Kaye could see him now, wandering among the trees as Allan often did, and it made her want to cry.

'You can leave him, you know, if he's treating you badly.'

Suddenly hearing her aunt's soft voice Kaye couldn't see for tears.

'He isn't treating me badly.' It was true. Allan wasn't beating her or drinking, at least not to any extent. He was even working. In fact his work was coming between them as he stayed more and more in chambers. Could neglect be called bad treatment? She didn't think so.

'He's making you very unhappy and we're both concerned for you. You could always come to us just for a little while. Allan's not the man he was, I know we talked about him seeing a doctor—'

'He wouldn't listen.' Kaye laughed shortly. 'I'm beginning to think that it's Allan who's sane and the rest of us have run mad.'

'I don't understand.'

'He sees things as they are. Allan sees reality. Other people make things up, live on their dreams, hope for better things for the future but there is no better with Allan, his cold light of day is never ending. I don't think he loves me. I think he regrets ever having married me.'

'Don't you regret it?'

'Certainly I do but I loved him then and I thought he loved me.'

Had the war ruined their marriage or had its ruination been born in its beginning? She didn't know. All she knew was that Allan never really came home any more. Why should he? There was nothing for him here.

'Come to us,' her aunt urged.

'I cannot.' She knew that it was stupid but somehow she had to be there, just in case Allan ever decided to come back. Was that love? It must be. But then what else could she do with her life?

Fourteen

Lilian Coulthard tried not to think about Jake. She thanked God for her good fortune and tried to be grateful. Her life was better now than it had been at any time and that included when she had been married. Jake's father had helped her to get a job but they had not invited her to their house, he had not introduced her to his wife and she knew that they were looking after Jake. His father even suggested that he had found her a job so that she could look for a more suitable place to live when the war was over because Jake would want his house, except that he didn't.

When Jake came home he came to see her and he was so thin and white-faced that Lilian longed to make dinners and say nice things but she made herself be polite and not offer because she could see how careful he was. He insisted that she should stay in his house while he was living with his parents, it would not be forever and when he wanted to come back there they would find her somewhere else to live. In the meanwhile what was the use in her moving out?

She had not expected to see him at work. She hadn't thought about that but she had a lot to do with Jake. This made Lilian very happy. She tried not to even think of him by his first name in case she slipped up and called him by it but she didn't.

She very correctly called him Mr Armstrong and he called her Mrs Coulthard and she got to know quite a bit about the Ballantine case because Jake was going to take it on in the court and he and Mr Fortnum, the man she worked directly for, were always having meetings and she felt involved even when she didn't see him.

Occasionally he would call in at the house on Saturdays and though she tried not to she began to wait for him to appear. She told herself that it was stupid, he never said he would call in and very often he didn't and it was her day off, so she would make herself go out, take Nora to the park but very often the weather was awful, sleet and wind, so it was too cold to take Nora out except for necessities.

Lilian made sure that she did her shopping during the week because Mr Fortnum insisted on her taking an hour at midday and she would call back at the house and make sure everything was all right with Nora and the woman who looked after her.

Seeing Jake at the house was quite different from seeing him at work. He was like another person, much more informal in his manner and dress, and he always said that he hoped she didn't mind and one Saturday it was like spring it was so nice and when he called she said she had just been going to take Nora out for a walk and he said he was sorry he had stopped her or interrupted and then she was bold enough to say, 'Well, why don't you come with us, if you would like, Mr Armstrong?'

She held on to her breath in case Jake should turn her down because if he did she would know that he was not really interested in her but was just doing his bit because he had known her husband and was sorry for what had happened but he seemed to think it was a very good idea.

It was a wonderful day. Lilian wished you could press such days between the leaves of books like you could with flowers so that she could have hung on to that day for a bit longer, it went by so fast. They walked along the towpath and when Nora grew tired, as she soon did, Jake carried her and they talked and the snowdrops were out and people were rowing on the river.

They went as far as Pelaw Woods and she began to wish they would never turn back, that somehow you could just keep on going forever. The sun twinkled through the trees and it was just as though the war had never been, nothing had happened.

On the way back they stopped and sat outside a little cafe and Jake bought tea and they had toasted teacake and Nora sat on his knee and dropped teacake all over him and Lilian thought it was the most precious day of her life.

It was late afternoon when they went back and he said he really must go and she said she was sorry she had kept him so late, she hadn't meant to. Jake was going out to dinner. He was going to his cousin's.

Lilian didn't understand how Jake and Mr Jamieson, who was defending Lady Ballantine, could go on being friends when they were on opposite sides in the courtroom but Jake said it wasn't like that and he and Kaye had always been fond of one another and that he had always known Allan, they had gone to school together and to Oxford and then to war. He was closer to them than anybody.

The day was ruined after he had gone. Lilian was almost sick with jealousy. No doubt lots of smart people would be at the dinner party. She had never been to such a thing.

There would be beautiful women wearing gorgeous frocks and there would be lovely things to eat and maybe Jake would meet somebody he really liked and decide to get married. She wished she could want him to meet somebody he really liked and get married but she couldn't unless it was going to be her and that wasn't very likely.

She found herself, having put Nora to bed, crying for her husband and for herself, for the loneliness of other people going to dinner parties and having a good time.

She tried not to think like that, she had been luckier than most but the evenings were so long and dark on her own and she didn't have any friends she could invite to spend time with her and she couldn't go anywhere because she left Nora all week during the day and she didn't think it was right to go out at night, though where she would have gone she couldn't think.

Jake had never liked Kaye and Allan's dinner parties. He knew that Allan didn't like them either but Kaye seemed so aware of her social position – Allan was rich. He was one of the richest men in the area and younger than the rest – and Allan's family had been so well thought of that she obviously deemed it a necessity. He didn't like to say no, even though he would much rather have stayed with Lilian.

It was almost as though Nora was his. He knew that he

107

was the nearest thing she had to a father. She ran to him when he came in the door, put out her arms to be picked up, cooed over him, put her tiny chubby hands into his hair. Jake loved her so much he had to keep on reminding himself that she was another man's child, the opposite argument being of course that the other man was dead.

He would have given so much to have stayed there with Lilian, to have gone to bed with her, woken up with her, had Sunday dinner, sat over the fire with Nora in his arms on Sunday afternoons. He desperately wanted normality.

He told himself it was just that he missed Madeline but he had to force himself to leave, to go home and change and go to Kaye and Allan's and try to be sociable. He had never felt less like going anywhere and they had such stupid friends. Allan didn't like any of them, Jake knew, but Kaye was doing her best and Jake felt obliged to be there and to be polite and to say the right things, even though they always invited the most unsuitable women to partner him.

Halfway through the evening he managed to get Kaye alone and say to her, 'Next time you do this could you ask Lilian Coulthard?'

Kaye looked at him. The others had gone through into the drawing room and she was just putting out the candles on the dining table. She hesitated.

'What, the young woman who lives in your house?'

'That's right.'

'Wouldn't people talk?'

'What do you mean?'

'Well . . . she has a child and you . . . don't be silly, Jake, you know exactly what I mean. People have already wondered why you provided her with your house. There would be a great deal of gossip.'

Jake stared at her.

'Her husband was in my battalion. I knew him. He was killed. She had nowhere to go. What was I supposed to do?'

'She could move somewhere else, couldn't she? She works.'

'There's no reason for her to move somewhere else,' Jake said.

108

'If she had an ounce of delicacy she would for the sake of your reputation,' Kaye said.

'That's not very nice, Kaye.'

Kaye faltered.

'I don't know how to say this to you without being offensive and you know I don't mean it personally but Lilian is coloured.'

'Don't be a bitch.'

'I'm not. It isn't me. Honestly, Jake, I would do whatever you wanted but please think carefully about this. Whatever would your parents say? And they've done so much for all of us. It hasn't been easy for them and they have lost Madeline and the baby too.'

'I like her.'

'Do you know what people would call her if you spent time with her and then it didn't work out?'

'What do you mean?'

'Don't be silly, Jake, she's a working-class girl, probably illegitimate, from the docks in Newcastle. They would call her your whore. Then she would lose her job and everything and she has a small child to keep. Have you thought of that?' Kaye waited for his reply and when Jake couldn't think of anything she put out the candles went off into the drawing room to attend to her guests.

After dinner Jake went outside into the garden and lit a cigarette. He didn't trust himself to be civil to the other guests, least of all the young woman they had invited for his sake who was so very pretty and had such a gorgeous figure that Jake had spent most of the evening imagining himself doing exquisitely dirty things to her. When the door opened behind him he half thought she had come out to him and he was going to have to get back inside or his worse self would determine to kiss her at the very least.

It was Allan.

'Thank God,' Jake said.

'What do you mean?'

'I thought you were the gorgeous Miss Sharp. I wish Kaye would stop dredging up women for me. Coming here is such a trial these days.'

'Don't you like her, then?'

'Of course I don't like her. She agreed with every comment I made and is about as interesting as last week's *Advertiser*.'

'You shouldn't put down the local paper like that, Jake,' Allan said and made him laugh.

'Couldn't you talk to Kaye about it?' Jake said.

'Kaye isn't the kind of person you can talk to any more,' Allan said and he didn't look at Jake.

'I noticed. She doesn't seem very happy. Is everything all right?'

There was a strange little pause before Allan said, 'I came back to my wife. You didn't.'

'That stops you telling me?'

Allan shrugged.

'It's just the war,' he said. 'She says I'm not the same person. It wasn't unbearable until Madeline died. After that I knew you didn't care much about anything and . . . I didn't either. I was terrified you weren't going to make it. There would have been nothing left.'

'There's Laurie,' Jake said.

'He feels like Kaye's child, not mine.'

Jake hesitated.

'I took Lilian Coulthard and Nora out for tea today.'

'That was nice,' Allan said.

'I asked Kaye to invite her here.'

'And she wouldn't?' Allan guessed. 'Not one of us, you see. Like Erin Ballantine. Kaye doesn't believe in people marrying out of their class, however she talks about education and opportunity for everybody.'

'I like her.'

'Do you? Are you sure it isn't the child that you like, almost the same age as yours would have been?'

'Maybe. The situation. It's difficult to divorce one from another. I think of her there in my house almost as Madeline.'

'The only way to find out would be if she moved.'

'I don't want her to move,' Jake said.

Fifteen

Diana Ballantine had been staying with friends so Allan got another chance to look at the house when she came back and he went to see her again. She seemed to have no worries about living there after what had happened and seemed comfortable with the idea that it would be sold when Erin did what she called 'paying for the awful thing she did'. The house would then be hers, of course. Was she motivated by this in what she said?

'You're convinced she did it?'

She hesitated.

'Mr Jamieson, I know that by now having seen her you could not possibly believe that such a beautiful woman killed her husband but beauty has very little to do with these things.'

That was not true, Allan thought, beauty was a very powerful force between people though Sir Angus, being blind had probably cared for Erin's youth and innocence. He had wanted her, it was as clear as that, and they had both paid for that misguided desire.

'It's not up to me to decide anything,' he said.

'I suspect you will defend her the better for thinking her not guilty. And no doubt you think the jury will be swayed by her.'

Allan remembered this later. Swayed by her. He certainly was. He stayed late at the office every night to avoid going home. The dull winter weather had set in, foggy frozen mornings and dull short afternoons.

He sat over the chambers' fire and drank whisky as he was not supposed to at home. No, that was silly, he thought, but Kaye would press her lips together when he drank anything other than tea as though the alcohol was making things worse, as though things could get any worse.

111

It seemed to him that Kaye no longer expected him home for dinner and would heat food on a plate when he finally got there. The first couple of times he didn't go back he could see the doused candles, the formally laid dining table. The smell of cold dinner would greet him at the door and Kaye would have nothing to say to him.

Sometimes as he was sitting down to eat she would go to bed so that she did not lose her temper with him. Allan was beyond caring. It felt to him as though Kaye was in league with her aunt and uncle, a conspiracy which had decided he was not a sane person, so he kept away.

One freezing February night when he was all alone in chambers he heard the outer door and when he went to investigate Erin Ballantine stood in the doorway. He was struck once again by how beautiful she was, her face pale from the cold and a dark coat hugged around her, her eyes sparkling in spite of how awful things were and the look of distress on her face which he would have given anything to remove.

'It wasn't locked,' she said, hovering there in the shadows.

'I always forget. Mrs Semple left hours ago and somehow . . . is something wrong?'

'Oh, Mr Jamieson, I don't think I can stand any more. I'm so afraid and I'm living there with my parents and there's nowhere to go and nothing to do and . . .'

Allan urged her indoors, gave her whisky, took her coat when she had warmed up a bit and he had built up the fire. He had been trying to decide whether to put on more coal or whether to give in and go home and since he was beyond making a decision the room was cooling but then so was any inclination he might have had to venture outside in such weather.

There in the lamplight she was even more beautiful than she had seemed before.

'They're going to hang me. I'm not twenty-one yet. I don't want to die.'

'I'm not going to let that happen,' he said.

He took hold of her hands. She had been wearing gloves but they were still very cold.

'It'll be all right, I promise you.' It was what she needed

to hear. What was the point in her losing sleep over it as well as him?

She smiled slightly.

'When you tell me that I believe you but when I don't see you it's difficult to go on believing it. I can't go out, people look at me in the street and it's so awful for my mam and dad. Folk talk and my mam gets upset and my dad goes to the pub like he never did before and . . .'

'Here, drink your whisky,' Allan said, handing it to her but she didn't. She leaned forward and she put her arms around his neck and kissed him and then drew back and said, 'Oh, I'm so sorry. I didn't mean to do that.'

'It's all right.'

'It's just that . . . I never met anybody like you before and I feel as if you're the only person who can help me. My future depends on you.'

'It's fine, really.'

'I love to hear you say that. I could spend the rest of my life listening to your voice. I wish that we had met before.'

'Before what?'

'Before I met Angus but then . . . you're married. How long?'

'Ten years.'

'I've seen your wife. She's very beautiful.'

'Yes.'

'She's very lucky.'

'She doesn't think so.'

'I wish I had known you then.'

'That wouldn't have been terribly suitable since you were probably about ten. I don't think relationships of that sort between men and children are generally assumed to be correct.'

She laughed.

'You are quite old, then,' she said, looking solemnly at him.

'I am, yes.'

'At least thirty?'

'A lot more than that.'

She hesitated and then she said, 'But you do like me?'

'Certainly.'

'And you do think I'm pretty?'

'I think you are astonishingly beautiful.'

'Astonishingly?'

'Very much so.'

She kissed him again and this time Allan gathered her to him in a way in which he had promised himself he wouldn't night after night in the darkness. He would be professional here, her life was at stake and he had never ever done such a thing before.

He did not tell himself that that was because he had had Kaye's love to shield him, Kaye's body to hide against in the long darkness. There was nowhere to hide any more and he was desperate to be hidden. It wouldn't have been so bad, he thought afterwards, if it had been nothing but a kiss but of course it wasn't.

Fuelled by whisky, silence and the protection of the great cathedral somehow, like the building was standing between himself and the world, almost in a stupid way as though it had its arm around him, Allan took the girl to him there in his room, put her down onto the rug before the fire and had her quite simply while she told him that she loved him and it was exquisite. It was possibly the most wonderful thing which had ever happened to him.

It was bold he thought but perhaps it was no more bold than for her to come to him there with this in mind as he had known she had. She told him she had loved no one before him. He wished he could have done the same. He wished he could have been twenty again and in love. And then he didn't. He had always loved Kaye and it was so bitter.

If Erin had killed Angus because the love between them was gone he understood perfectly and he didn't blame her. His sober self told him that it was nothing like that. The barrister which remained gave a whole pile of other arguments but it didn't make any difference and Allan took comfort from that.

He was happy as he had not been happy in years in the firelight with the girl and the golden whisky. He told her that he loved her as though telling would make it so or perhaps it already was or maybe it was just that he was as good as

114

the world at fabricating lies and hope when in fact all he had were those moments.

She gave herself so sweetly, so completely. Only when it was very late did she say to him, 'Is this right?'

'Do you mean is it ethical between lawyer and client or morally wrong because I'm married?'

'I don't know. I only know . . .' She looked at him. 'You're the only person who can help me and I want to be near in every possible sense so that I might understand you.'

Allan wasn't convinced of this argument. Being close to Kaye hadn't helped the understanding of his marriage or perhaps it was the lack of physical closeness which had damaged it so much. Whatever, he didn't care. He took her into his arms and then over to the old sofa at the back of the room. Things would never be the same again, he thought, and he didn't care.

'Is Allan in?'

Kaye opened the door herself. It was Fiona the parlour-maid's evening off. Mary should have been around but she wasn't. Fiona had a young man, what in the old days they would have called a follower, and sometimes they were not allowed. Nowadays, Kaye thought with a sigh, nothing would stop any girl from reaching for any young man who took an interest in her. She didn't blame them.

Did anybody have any restraint left when men were so scarce? Certainly Fiona had swelled with pride when she announced to Kaye that she would be going out that evening if that was all right and Kaye had said that of course she must go. There was no reason to keep the girl there.

Kaye let Jake in.

'Did you want to speak to him especially? I expect he's still in chambers. He's always there.'

She stopped and indicated that Jake should have the sofa and then sat down in an armchair to one side of the fire.

'You were so pale when I was over last week and Allan is so silent. I just thought I might be able to help,' Jake said.

'Darling Jake, whatever makes you think that?'

'Would you like me to talk to him?'

'And say what?'

115

'That he's making you unhappy.'

'I'm sure he knows that already. Do you think he will go on with the Ballantine case?'

'He seems very keen.'

Kaye looked down at her fingers.

'If you're prosecuting this case and he's defending we don't need any more complications, surely.'

'That's work, Kaye.'

'I know. I don't understand how you can be so objective.'

'It goes with the job.'

Jake tried to reassure her but he could not help thinking about Jonnie Fieldgate. They had gone to school together, gone to war. He had come back, one of the few who made it all the way through, and then disappeared. His family had no idea where he was and it had been a year now and there was no sign of him. He had been so cheerful for four bloody years.

'I feel like I'm married to someone I've just met. I can't ...' She looked across the fire at him. She didn't say 'someone I don't love' but her gaze was full of apology. 'You have the most awful way of making people tell you things.'

Jake understood, or he thought he did. Allan had come back from war a different person and assumed that his wife would go to bed with him and he was so altered that she no longer wanted to, or did Allan not want to? Jake wasn't sure. Some of the men had had girls in France, even though they were not supposed to. War made you do stupid things. He didn't know about Allan, had he been faithful to Kaye?

Jake didn't see the alteration in Allan personally. No more than himself. After Madeline's death he had spent the rest of the war doing what Allan had called 'trying your damnedest to get killed'. Allan had actually rescued him personally once, Jake fighting him off all the time and swearing at him horribly afterwards. Some bloody guardian angel he made, Jake thought now, in reluctant admiration.

Allan had had so much to live for. He had a wife and child, Laurie had been just a little boy when he went away.

Strangely enough, Jake thought now, his own desire for

116

death hadn't worked. People had called him brave, he had been given medals, but it was cowardice, he knew it was. He hadn't wanted to go on.

Jake knew that really brave people put such things behind them and married again and had other children but somehow he couldn't. He had an almost overwhelming desire to tell Kaye how lucky she was that Allan had come home but he knew that it was a stupid thing to say. Allan hadn't come home. His youth had been lost in the horrors of France and Kaye was left with nothing but a shell for a husband.

He left Kaye and decided to go to chambers. He expected it to be quiet and he wanted to think and in a way he wanted to get away from the kindness of his parents who had been pretending for so long that everything would be all right that it had become a way of life.

Not that he thought they were wrong to do so, he admired it. What else were people to do and his parents were not the kind of people to let life better them. He admired it but sometimes he needed to get away from it and tonight he did.

He wished he could call on Lilian but it was getting late and that would look bad and besides he felt as if he mustn't go there. Every time he saw her he wanted to hold her and that wouldn't be right or fair.

He liked the city streets when they were so quiet. It was late enough that even the drunks and whores had gone home. He wandered his way down to Framwellgate Bridge and across it and then up the narrow winding way which was Silver Street, into the Market Place and then up Saddler Street.

To go to his chambers he would cross Elvet Bridge but if he had been going home to Madeline he would have gone left through the Market Place and toiled up the steep bank that was Claypath and there was a small bit of his mind which would not let him away from the thought that somewhere in another time Madeline was waiting for him in the pretty house where they had been so happy. He could not quite believe she was not there.

He didn't cross the Bridge or go through the Market Place towards home, he decided instead to go up to Palace Green and see what the cathedral looked like by moonlight. The

117

bank became steep just before you went around the corner into Owengate and then he stopped.

Some way in front of him a man and a woman were in an embrace. He moved back slightly but silently. They looked as though they were saying goodnight. Even then there was no mistake. They could not have known anybody was there or they would not have held one another so close and in such a good light but it was late and why should they suspect anybody they knew would be watching? Because Jake had known him all his life he could see Allan. The woman was Erin Ballantine.

They began to walk arm in arm towards him. Jake slipped back into the shadows, further and further and then he walked backwards, very carefully in case he should slip, fall and alert them to his presence and when he had walked back down Saddler Street far enough so that he thought they could not hear him he turned and ran.

He ran all the way back to his parents' house like a child who has fallen down and skinned his hands, back down the steep cobbles of Saddler Street and through the Market Place where everything was silent and down the twisting narrowness of Silver Street and across Framwellgate Bridge from where the cathedral and castle could be clearly seen, one of the most famous views in the country.

South Street was just off to the left at the far side and it was very hard to climb but he didn't let it govern his pace. He halted just outside the door, not wanting to burst in. They might be asleep and either way he did not want to disturb them. He had caused them enough grief in his life already.

He went upstairs as quietly as he could and into his bedroom. He had not realized how cold he was until then. The fire burned as it always did. He was grateful to his mother and Mrs Gainsborough, the housekeeper, for their efficiency. There was also food on a tray and wine but Jake made his way over to the brandy decanter which stood on the dressing table with a silver tray beneath it.

Mrs Gainsborough knew there were times when men needed brandy. No doubt she was used to his father. She was right, Jake thought now, going over and pouring far too much into a glass. How did women know these things?

118

He sat down by the fire in possibly the most comfortable chair in the world but his hands shook as he put the brandy glass to his lips. After a while the shaking steadied but it was difficult not to call Allan names, not to think how stupid he was, not to consider Allan greedy, he already had a wife at home. What did he need with Erin?

And then Jake thought back. Erin was beautiful. She was not Allan's responsibility, at least she was but not from any marital standpoint. She was not the mother of his child. She was not waiting at home for him and most importantly of all she had not known what he was like before. She accepted him as he was now.

Jake thought he would have given almost anything in the world that somebody like Kaye should be waiting at home for him with his child. How could Allan want so much? But then perhaps it was because too many people settled for so little. He had. He had settled for sanity – was that so little? – and the idea that the mornings would arrive. It was pathetic, Jake decided.

Allan could come back from war and take another woman into his arms. Was it brave, foolhardy or just a demonstration to God that he could be the kind of bastard that other men had died and not been? And what about Laurie? What would happen now?

Jake drank too much brandy and fell into bed but it meant that he didn't think any more.

In the morning he was too busy to go and see Allan but he cancelled his lunch engagement and had his clerk send a note to Allan's chambers and then he went across. Allan was quiet. Was he always as quiet as this, Jake thought, or had his relationship with Erin Ballantine done it?

Once the door was closed Jake said, 'I saw you last night.'

Allan looked at him and Jake, who had grown used to those cold grey eyes during the past few years, said, 'With the woman you're defending.'

'So?'

'So you were kissing her.'

There was silence. Somebody talked excitedly beyond the window. Outside, people were walking up to the cathedral on the narrow cobbled street which twisted up towards Palace Green or on the even narrower pavement as they always did. In the room all Allan said was, 'And?'

Jake hated his self-containment.

'It isn't . . .' What, ethical? Allan would laugh. Morally correct? Allan would laugh even more, Jake could see just by looking at him. 'What about Kaye?'

Allan smiled. Jake hated his smile.

'Kaye doesn't want me. I'm not betraying her. She wants somebody I used to be or wasn't, somebody she's made up for herself or believes from books. I don't know. I can't be that person. I don't know how to be any more. I don't think I ever did.'

'Don't you love Kaye?'

'I don't know.'

'But you're in love with Erin Ballantine?'

Allan laughed. Jake hit him. He couldn't help it, he couldn't bear the laughter. He was so angry with Allan for making such a mess of something which should have been all right. Allan and Kaye had been all Jake had had left with regard to couples, the only thing to look up to somehow, and also he thought of the waste. If Madeline had still been alive they would have been together in the house by the river with their baby. Allan and Kaye were alive with their child. How could they do this to one another?

He was half convinced that Allan had known he was about to hit him. They both had so much experience of such things. Allan could have stopped anybody from hitting him had he cared to so perhaps he didn't care about being knocked across the room. Allan even looked at him with sympathy so maybe he knew what Jake was thinking, how upset he was because the last thing he had believed in had gone wrong and Allan was apparently to blame.

Jake could hear the rush of feet beyond the door as the noise reached other people. He leaned back against the door and when Allan's clerk said, 'Is everything all right, Mr Jamieson?' he stood until Allan wiped his bleeding mouth and said from the floor, 'Everything's fine.'

Only when the silence had proceeded from beyond the

120

door and Mr Roscommon had obviously gone away did Jake say, 'You have a wife and child. Is nothing enough?'

Allan got to his feet as though nothing had happened and then he said, 'No, nothing's enough any more.'

Jake watched him but Allan said, 'I'm sorry, Jake, I can't be like you. It isn't a life you're leading, it's just an existence. You don't go anywhere or see anybody or do anything. Madeline's dead. When are you going to get past that?'

Jake didn't answer. Then he said slowly, 'I'm beginning to think I never shall get past it. Maybe I'm just jealous.'

Allan's shoulders slumped.

'I used to think what it would be like, you know, when I came home but it isn't like that.'

'No, I know.'

'Erin is new, you see. She doesn't expect anything.'

'She expects you to save her.'

'I don't think she does and besides, I will.'

'Allan, she did it.'

'You don't know that.'

'Yes, I do, and so do you.'

Allan's eyes mocked him.

'This from a man who used to boast that he could kill a man he could barely see. Don't give me petty morality, it's just the same thing. You've killed dozens, maybe hundreds of people, and so have I. Erin may have killed one. Do you think she didn't have good reason for it? Do you think he wasn't a bastard like the rest of us? What does it matter to you or to me?'

'It matters because we make it our business.'

'Hypocritically.'

'Maybe. Are you telling me he treated her badly?' He looked clearly at Allan.

'Perhaps. She hasn't said so, in fact she's denied it. I don't care. I don't care what she did.'

'And are you going to go from Erin back to your wife?'

Allan laughed. He laughed with a kind of amusement that made Jake want to leave.

'You still don't understand, do you, or don't you choose to? Kaye doesn't want me. I haven't been in my wife's bed

121

in two years. I'm sorry if you find that crude but it's the truth. She hates the person I've become, the man who . . .' Allan stopped there, just when Jake thought he had a good hold on the subject. 'She despises me,' he said.

There was something honest about it and Jake thought, yes, Allan had come back from war ready to envelop his wife in his arms but there was blood on his hands, death in his mind, the futility of life all around him. Maybe she could even smell the graves on him, the dead bones of all those dead men, the rotting flesh.

Maybe, Jake thought, honest with himself at last, the same thing might have happened between himself and Madeline, instead of which he had this perfect image to look back on, his wonderful marriage, everything falling down beside it, nothing to endanger the memories, like a scrapbook or a photograph album, everything neat, nothing disturbed.

'I'll prove she killed him,' Jake said, 'and she'll hang.'

Allan looked pityingly at him.

'Why don't you just go, or I'll give you such a hiding as you never had in your life.'

He meant it too, Jake thought, moving away. Perhaps, he thought as he left, you never get to mourning, perhaps the shock of losing the person you loved most in the world is so bad that the grief is never-ending.

Who thought of the idea that there is mourning and that there are stages of it which you accomplish? Some idiot who knew nothing. Perhaps an optimist, somebody who has never been through such a thing, some churchman, some celibate, somebody childless.

A person who thinks you come back from the lonely place where loss put you. It was not true, he thought. And now he was childless and celibate. How strange. Like the world had nothing at all to do with him nor he with it any more.

Worse still his parents wanted to move on. No, he corrected himself, they wanted to move him on and they were so careful of him and so caring that it was difficult to refuse. His mother came to him tentatively that day with the idea that they might have a party.

'That sounds nice,' Jake said.

The morning room, painted buttercup yellow at his mother's insistence – it was horrible to contemplate first thing in the morning, he had to admit, especially if you'd been drinking the night before – was full of sunlight that day. He looked at her across the table and thought how much he loved her.

'It's our wedding anniversary,' she said.

'Which one?'

'Forty years.'

'Good heavens,' Jake said.

She looked shyly at him.

'We were married for some time before we had you. We had almost given up hope and then you altered our lives forever. So we are going to invite all our friends and have a huge party.'

'How lovely,' Jake said. 'Can we invite Lilian Coulthard?'

His mother hesitated.

'She has a little girl, doesn't she?'

'People who have children still go to parties,' Jake said gently.

His mother put a hand on his hand.

'You will marry again and have children of your own. You won't need other people's.'

'Don't you like her?'

'I'm sure she's a charming girl but . . . if you are to go forward in your life and your profession, you need a suitable wife. I don't mean to be nasty.'

'Was Madeline suitable?'

'She was a lot more suitable than Mrs Coulthard.'

'I thought you had reservations.'

'Madeline was different but she was intelligent, her parents were educated. What do we know of Lilian Coulthard? Only that she was probably illegitimate, that she was obliged to get married, that she is a coloured girl—'

'I like her,' Jake said.

His mother sighed.

'I don't understand why you can't be satisfied with a woman on your own social level. Goodness knows there are hundreds of them without husbands—'

'I just like Lilian,' Jake said.

'I'm very sorry about that,' his mother said, 'but I certainly won't be inviting her here.'

Sixteen

Nell had come to her nervously but Kaye could not help thinking that there was a distasteful triumph about it. Nell's husband had given her three children. He was faithful to her, devoted even. They had lots of money, a beautiful house in South Street, though not, Kaye thought in one of her worse moments, a better house than her own. This was one of the most beautiful houses in the area and perhaps Nell was jealous.

She was certainly jealous of Nell, who owned expensive jewellery. Her husband bought her a new piece every birthday, every anniversary, every Christmas. They went on wonderful holidays, they both had affectionate parents. Nell had everything, Kaye thought, gritting her teeth as Nell proceeded to tell her that the whole town was talking about Allan and Lady Ballantine.

Kaye was mortified, astounded, wished more than anything that at least her mother had been there. Nell's mother was so kind, Nell had plenty of places to run to when things went wrong.

Kaye went to the only place she had, Jake's mother. She too appeared to know what was going on.

'You must leave Allan, Kaye,' her aunt said, 'I told you before.'

'Leave him?'

Her aunt looked pained.

'Surely you know what people are saying? I know, I know,' she put up a hand as Kaye began to protest, 'one should never listen to gossip but there's more to it. People are talking about him and his connection with Erin Ballantine and even if there's nothing in it and I don't think for a moment there is, this . . . connection is the result of the unhappiness which

124

has been growing for a very long time. You should have left him months ago, my dear.'

Kaye hadn't realized until then how much Jake's mother disliked Allan but she could remember when they were small and Allan's parents had died that her aunt would not have him to stay during the school holidays when Jake came home.

Allan had always, from being seven, been sent to London to stay with distant relatives in the holidays even though Jake was forever asking whether he could come to stay. She remembered her aunt making excuses, that she already had a child, that Kaye and Reggie spent a great deal of time there because their mother was not well.

Her aunt, Kaye thought, had a lot on her hands, a dying sister and a niece and nephew about to become orphaned. She didn't want another responsibility and Allan had been so very quiet and distant as a little boy, she thought.

She remembered when he had come back to Durham when he had finished at Oxford and London and he was tall, well mannered, quiet, with cool dark eyes. The house in Durham belonged to other people by then but Hedleyhope House was ready and waiting for him.

She had fallen in love with him the moment they met as adults. Allan was the kind of man waiters instinctively went to first because although he didn't say a great deal he could do what her uncle called 'making his presence felt'. Allan had great presence and it frightened people. He could always find you a seat in a crowded room. Allan, Kaye thought, had been so good at war. Other men said he was a real leader. And he expected to be obeyed, he didn't consider that anybody else might know better.

It had not mattered so much when he had loved her but, Kaye thought with a sigh, that had been a very long time ago. Allan had belonged to her. She thought of the first time he had come back from France and she had been shocked at how cold and silent he had become but it was always there. He was always putting himself away from people but then he was so intelligent and so rich that it did not encourage friendships but the mothers of the district had got very

125

enthusiastic when Allan had first come home to practise law and they thought of their daughters marrying him.

Kaye's aunt and uncle were very proud when she landed Allan, she thought, wincing. Men were jealous of him, men on his social and financial level. Perhaps that was why he had been good in war, because of the men beneath him that he could be friends with. Was that it?

'You really think he's having an affair?' Until then Kaye had not put the matter into words.

'I don't know. That dreadful poisonous woman, she would obviously do anything to get what she wants.'

'What about Laurie?'

'Don't you think Laurie would be better without Allan's influence?'

Kaye tried to remember this conversation in full but as she fled home and up the stairs and began to cry hard behind the safety of her bedroom door all she knew was that she did not want to leave, she did not want to talk to Allan about this, she did not even want to acknowledge that he might have someone else and she hated Erin Ballantine for being so beautiful and for wanting Allan.

Allan and Kaye came to the anniversary party at Jake's parents' house. Jake did not tell his parents that he and Allan had quarrelled. Kaye looked pale. Allan acknowledged Jake politely at the beginning of the party and then said nothing more.

Halfway through the evening Jake managed to detach him from the crowd he had surrounded himself with and lead him off into the library. Allan allowed himself to be led.

Allan however said nothing and Jake remembered how stubborn and determined Allan had been in the war. The men had loved him because he looked after them, he would push and push to get everything for them, would brave his commanders to try and better things and encourage by word and example. He had been a brilliant leader because of these qualities. The personal cost, Jake thought, had been huge.

Allan didn't say anything, just wandered the room as though he hadn't been used to it all his life.

'And how is Lady Ballantine?' Jake asked.

126

'Oh, bugger off, Jake,' Allan said tiredly, lighting a cigarette, and Jake glanced at the door but it was shut.

'I just don't know what to say to you.'

'You don't have to say anything to me. We can do all our talking in court.'

'Are you going to tell Kaye or are you going to wait until somebody else does?'

'I don't care.'

'You've loved her for most of your life.'

'Why isn't Lilian Coulthard here?'

Jake was taken aback, firstly because Allan changed the subject so abruptly from something he had no intention of discussing and secondly because it was exactly what he thought himself and nobody else seemed to care about. Why should Allan care after all that had gone on between them? Yet he did.

'My mother didn't want her here.' Allan looked at him. 'I've put them through such a lot,' Jake said, 'I married to please myself once. They never liked Madeline and it was hard for them when she died . . . and the child . . . They've been so good to me.'

'Is it the little girl you love?'

Straight to the point as always, Jake thought.

'Nora. I want my child so much.'

'I know.'

'And my life. The life I had. I suppose you can say that of us all, we all want back what we had and none of us can. I'm sorry I hit you, that's what I wanted to say. I didn't mean to go around being judgemental, but . . .'

'Oh, forget it, I don't care.'

'But what about you and Kaye?'

'Kaye doesn't love me any more, it's quite simple,' Allan said.

'It's not simple!' Jake didn't realize he had raised his voice until after he spoke. 'It isn't simple, Allan, you know it isn't.'

'I miss her, you know,' Allan said. 'I used to think we all – we had everything.'

'We did have everything. Now we've lost it. Our parents should have told us it wasn't going to last.'

'Mine weren't here to do it and yours, they still have

everything, so how can they possibly understand? If you want Lilian Coulthard, Jake, for God's sake marry her. It's awful to know more than your parents do. Go ahead and take what you can.'

'I want to play Happy Families,' Jake said, with the ghost of a smile.

Have you got anything to drink in here?'

'Good brandy.'

'You have?' Allan looked relieved and when Jake poured it Allan even smiled at him across the big balloon glass and they sat there in leather armchairs and began to talk of something else.

Seventeen

When the trial began Erin looked the way that Allan had told her to look. She wore a simple blue dress which made her look even younger than she was. She did not come into court dressed like people imagined Lady Ballantine would dress though in fact she had not the clothes to do so in any case.

She looked the kind of woman every man would fall in love with and with good reason, her innocence. She wore no furs, no jewellery, no lipstick. She was, as his father would have said, 'as God made her', in the simple blue dress, her eyes full of dismay.

It was a long time since Allan had felt the need to protect anybody in the way that he felt now towards Erin Ballantine. He was confident that she would come out of this alive and cleared of any guilt. What would happen then he could not think.

She would not be able to keep on the house unless he and Kaye were divorced and they were married. His money would enable Erin to keep the house she loved. That made him feel uncomfortable. He tried to put to the back of his mind the idea that Erin might make use of him, perhaps was already doing so.

In the first days of the trial there were character witnesses, people who could tell the court about the people concerned in the affair. Jake dredged up people who had known and respected Sir Angus. Allan would produce Erin's employer, people from where she lived. There was in fact little hard evidence of any kind though he had sat in chambers night after night trying to work his way through what there was. Jake had the murder weapon and that was the main problem.

When you could produce a silver pistol in court the effect on the jury was substantial.

He wished there had been servants, somebody to overhear something which would help, somebody to see. The only servant they had had was a part-time chauffeur who had left well before the death so that was of no help.

The people actually involved because they were in the house at the time were Sir Angus, Erin and Diana. He knew that he would have to prove conclusively that she had not committed murder and for that he might be obliged to put her on the stand and he was determined not to do that but he held it in reserve for later, in case everything else should fail.

The first few days were exhausting. When he got home at the end of the fourth day Kaye's luggage was at the door. She came out of the drawing room as though she had been waiting.

'I'm leaving you,' she said.

What impeccable timing, Allan thought, going through into the dining room and pouring whisky from the decanter. It was one thing that had improved. She followed him into the room.

'I was under the impression that you were keen to keep appearances going,' he said.

'That was before the whole of Durham City knew that you were running around with a common little . . .'

Murderess? Bitch? Was Kaye really lost for words?

'I can't think why you didn't tell me,' she said.

'Is it important?'

She stared at him and if Allan had needed revenge for the way he blamed her over their marriage he would have gained it tenfold.

'You are sleeping with this woman?'

Allan looked at her.

'You're objecting?'

Kaye looked down.

'No,' she said finally. 'No, why would I? I just wish that you had managed to keep it quiet. I thought our marriage meant more to you than that.'

'Did you? I wonder why. Our marriage. We don't have a marriage any more, Kaye. Why go on with the charade?'

She didn't look at him at all and Allan found difficulty in

remaining in the room with her. He made himself not move. He drank deeply of the whisky he had poured.

'Would you like me to drive you to your aunt's, I presume that's where you're going?'

'You can't wait to get rid of me, can you? Tell me, what does she do for you that I haven't? Is it about sex?'

'Surely that's what everything's about,' Allan said.

'How can you say so?'

'It is.' And then he came to her and smiled and said, 'Oh, come on, Kaye, you don't want me. You haven't wanted me in a very long time. At least admit it. I repulse you.'

'You do not,' Kaye said, choking on tears.

'That's your respectability talking. You won't even let me sleep in the same room. Are you sleeping with Jake?'

Kaye stared at him.

'Of course I'm not. Whatever gave you such an idea?'

'You seem to like him so well.'

'He was your best friend and he's my cousin. Would it make you feel better if I said I did, then you needn't feel guilty any more?'

'I don't feel guilty.'

'Well, that's all right, then.'

'No, it isn't. I feel so many other things, there isn't room.'

'Like what?'

'Oh, hopelessness, defeat, completely out of time with everything. Let me take you into town.'

'Certainly not.'

'Don't let's behave like other people, eh? And perhaps you wouldn't . . .'

'Wouldn't what?'

'Fight with me over Laurie. I will do so if you make me but I don't want to put any of us through it.'

'I wouldn't do that to you, Allan. You may see him whenever you wish.'

Allan smiled at that.

'Considering he's two hundred and forty miles away in bloody London.'

'You went there.'

'I thought that might have stopped you from sending him.'

'I didn't send him. He had his name down—'

'That was your uncle's doing, not mine. I can't remember why I allowed it.'

'And what else was he to do? For goodness' sake, Allan, Laurie isn't you.'

'That's the only saving grace about this whole thing,' Allan said.

Kaye let Allan drive her to her aunt and uncle's house but would not allow him to stay once he had put her suitcases out of the car.

'I'll help you in with them, they're heavy.'

'I'm sure my uncle can carry them. I'd rather you didn't have to stay and see my aunt.'

'All right,' he said and went.

Kaye banged on the door and to her surprise Reggie answered it.

'Hello, Kaye, what's going on?' He eyed the suitcases.

'I've come for a visit. My aunt has asked me. Will you carry that lot in for me?' and Kaye walked into the hall.

Reggie did as he was asked, only saying when everything was inside and the door was shut, 'My uncle and aunt are not here.'

'Not here? Where are they?'

'In St Andrews playing golf. It's been planned for weeks. Had you forgotten?'

Kaye was so annoyed at herself for forgetting. Jake came through into the hall at that point. He also looked hard at the suitcases.

'My aunt asked me here.'

Jake reacted rather like Allan would have, she thought, typical barrister, practicalities first. He said, 'I'll have a room sorted out for you and then we can take your stuff upstairs. Have you eaten?'

'I don't want anything to eat, thank you,' Kaye said, rather inclined to cry now that she realized what she had done and she walked past them both into the sitting room.

Jake followed her in and closed the door. Kaye hovered by the fire.

'I didn't know they weren't going to be here or I wouldn't have come.'

'Have you quarrelled with Allan?'

She turned and looked at him.

'He's sleeping with the woman he's defending. I can't stay there any more.'

Jake said nothing to that.

'You knew?' Kaye said.

'Yes.'

'You might have told me.'

'I rather hoped it was just a . . . passing fancy.'

Kaye, fighting for control, turned back to the fire.

'Apparently not,' she said. 'Your mother said I could come here whenever I wanted to.'

'By all means. I'll sort things out. Would you like some tea or . . . or something stronger?'

'No, thank you, I'm fine.'

Jake left her there and a short time later Kaye was able to go to the room which had been prepared for her. The suitcases were all upstairs and she had a view which looked out across the river at the castle and the cathedral. It was a beautiful view, at least she supposed it must be, just like the main rooms downstairs but better but she couldn't see as she at last gave in to the tears she had been holding back all that day.

She didn't go back downstairs. Jake sent a maid to help her unpack and settle in and she had tea when she got into bed but she couldn't sleep. She kept turning over and over in her mind the way that her marriage had failed and how people would talk and then she wondered what would happen now that she had officially left. What would she say to Laurie?

She endured several hours of this before she couldn't stand any more and then she went across the hall and knocked on the door of Jake's room. He didn't answer. He must be in a deep sleep. She opened the door and walked in.

The curtains were pulled back and the room was full of shadows. She went over and sat down on the edge of the big bed and said his name.

'Jake?'

When he didn't say anything she touched him on the shoulder and in less than a second he had got hold of her, pulled her down on to the bed and had her helpless on her back with an arm across her throat. Then he stared and released her.

'God, I'm sorry. I got such a shock.'

Kaye sat up, rubbing her throat.

'Do you always react like that when people surprise you?'

'Not lately.'

He sat back too, letting go of his breath in a long sigh.

'What time is it?'

'I don't know, about three, I think.'

'I hate three o'clock in the morning,' Jake said, and he got up and lit the lamp on the bedside table. 'Can't sleep?' he guessed.

'No.'

'Should you have left Allan?'

Kaye glared at him in the lamplight.

'He's having an affair with another woman. What was I supposed to do?'

'Well,' Jake considered, 'looking at it from a legal standpoint you have a great deal to lose financially.'

'Surely I'm entitled to a large part of what he has. I'm his wife.'

'Possibly. Then again, possibly not.'

'I can divorce him for adultery, can't I?'

'Yes.'

'You sound doubtful.'

'I'm not doubtful about that part, it's just that I have the feeling Allan's financial interests are so many and so varied and so complicated and have been made safe for him for many years and I should think it would take a lot more than a failed marriage on his part for you to get your hands on anything substantial. Also . . .'

'Also what?'

'Allan's a slippery character.'

Kaye didn't have any argument with that.

'You know . . .' Jake said and then stopped.

'What?'

'Nothing.'

'Say it. It can hardly be any worse.'

But it was.

'A lot of women put up with their husbands behaving like that. They don't lose their tempers and then walk out.'

'I did not lose my temper!'

'You're losing it now,' Jake pointed out. 'You've got a lot more to lose if you don't go back to Allan, to say nothing of the fact that you have a child together. What about Laurie?'

'Your mother says—'

'Oh, damn my mother,' Jake said. 'She always has a blasted opinion about everything. She's never been in your position.'

'I can't go on living with him.'

'There are worse things.'

'Thank you, Jake, you're such a comfort.'

'There are. Think what living on your own would be like without Allan's money, influence and position in this town and how you would have to use Laurie like a shuttlecock between you. A divorced woman is not a social attribute to any dinner party whereas Allan would always be because of who he is and his money—'

'That is grossly unfair.'

'I didn't say it wasn't. You're going to be very lonely.'

'I'm already very lonely. I have been for the past five years. Allan is . . . is sleeping with a woman fifteen years younger than me. How do you think that makes me feel? She's stunning,' Kaye said and burst into tears.

It had not been part of Jake's plan that evening that he should end up in bed with Allan's wife while she wept into his pillows. They had slept together when they were children. He did not like to point out to her that they were not children now and . . . and what? Also he had been contemptuous of Allan sleeping with Erin Ballantine.

Kaye was all warm nightie and wet face, damp strands of hair sticking to her shiny cheeks as she finally emerged. She put her face against his bare shoulder and her arms around him.

'Kaye . . .'

'What?'

She obviously and very unflatteringly, Jake thought, considering he was wearing nothing except the bottom half of his father's striped pyjamas, was completely impervious to the situation and to any charms he thought he might still have had. And then she let go of him and said, 'Oh, don't be ridiculous, I'm not trying to get you to make love to me.'

'Well, that's a relief,' Jake said and she looked at him and they both laughed. And then Kaye stopped.

'She's taken my husband.'

'You made him available.'

'What do you mean?'

'You stopped sleeping with him, Kaye.'

'Why does it always come down to that. Allan was so—'

'Please, spare me the details,' Jake begged.

'I was so angry when he left to go to the war and every time he came back he was less and less the person I knew, the man who belonged to me. He belonged to the war and the men and even though his health has always been precarious he went on risking his life for people while I had to be content with crumbs. I wasn't proud when he got the VC, I felt so shut out. Isn't that awful?'

She was so close that Jake could smell the warmth of her body, see nothing beyond the way that her mouth was trembling, and her eyes had a wonderful blue shine. The tiny little straps of her nightdress had fallen from her shoulders on to her arms and he was losing the sense of what she was saying.

'It's . . . it's completely understandable,' he said.

'Do you think it is? Allan went away to war the man I adored and came back silent and bitter and cold. I couldn't love him any more.'

A tear slid over the ridge of her top lip and she reached out with the tip of her tongue and caught it.

'Jake?'

It was just a prompting so that he would say something intelligent, something compassionate. He had moved back. The pillows impeded any further retreat. They were hard

136

against the bedhead. Jake tried to think about work, about the case.

It was a beautiful nightdress, Kaye was a rich man's wife, however much she despised what he had become, and the nightdress was some expensive material, low with lace across her breasts and outlining the soft curves of her body in the palest of blue silk. Jake thought she was the most delectable thing he had ever set eyes on.

She was very close now, almost sitting on him. He couldn't hear what she was saying at all and there was very little space between them. She leaned forward ever so slightly and then he was kissing her. Her body hesitated as though in surprise and then she covered the tiny distance that remained and the full softness and warmth of her body overwhelmed him.

Kaye would have given a lot to have been back in her bed at Hedleyhope House. She would have given a lot to be anywhere but here. Daylight was sending a thin sliver of light across the carpet. They had barely slept. Jake was asleep now though, face down, his naked body so beautiful in the half light that Kaye shivered. What had she done?

It was almost incestuous, she thought. And then her sense of humour rescued her. Nothing in the world would ever have induced her to see Reggie in such a light. He and Jake were as unlike as they could possibly be.

She loved Reggie because he was her brother but very often she didn't like him at all, didn't admire the way that he behaved. She understood it. Reggie was still the little boy who had lost his parents. He had behaved in the very opposite way that Allan had behaved when he had lost his parents at much the same age. Allan had been independently minded ever since. Reggie had never learned to cope.

Thinking of Allan smote her with guilt. Not only had she gone to bed with her cousin, she had gone to bed with one of Allan's best friends. How very trite. She had, and she knew it was a cliché, taken advantage of Jake. She hadn't meant to.

When they had been small children they often slept together. Reggie was younger than she was and inclined to whine and very often when he fell asleep she would creep into Jake's room and slide into bed with him, just for reassurance.

He hadn't changed, he was still the perfect person to sleep with. He moved very little in his sleep but when he did it was to turn over and move in against you and put one arm around you in reassurance.

There was a used brandy glass on the bedside table near her. She could smell it. Could she leave without waking him? The second she moved he said distinctly, 'I'm not asleep.'

'Pretend?' she said hopefully and with a touch of humour and Jake lifted his head.

'There was nothing wrong with it,' he said.

'And you call yourself modest?'

He laughed softly and rather ruefully, she thought, as though he too regretted the night.

'I didn't mean it like that,' he said.

'I know you didn't, Jake, darling, I—' and that was as far as she got.

He pulled her across the bed into his arms.

'Don't do the guilt thing, eh?' he said.

'I always considered myself to be good.'

'Better than Allan?'

Kaye squirmed under the inference.

'Was that the point?' she said.

'Of course not,' he said and she saw the kindness in his eyes. 'It was only once.'

'That's what you call once?'

'One night. It was one night.'

'And if Allan only slept with Erin Ballantine once? Should I forgive him for that?'

'He doesn't love Erin Ballantine, Kaye, he went to her because you put him out of your bed.'

'I didn't want him.' Kaye tried to look anywhere but at him. 'I didn't think I wanted anybody.'

Jake looked at her for a second and then he kissed her, slowly and deliberately on the mouth. Kaye drew nearer and nearer until there wasn't nearer to be.

'That's not true, is it?' Jake said.

* * *

Kaye thought, later, when she could think again, that this was in a way just because he was Jake. She wouldn't dream of doing this . . . no, she hadn't dreamt of doing this with anyone but Allan, had thought she didn't want anyone any more but it wasn't true, he was right.

She was no better in her way than Erin Ballantine had been, it was just that she had married a rich young man instead of a poor disabled older one, but in its way her marriage had been just as difficult as anybody else's and if Erin Ballantine had shot her husband Kaye was beginning to see why people murdered one another.

She had felt like killing Allan when she had found out he was seeing another woman and apparently didn't care that people suspected him of it though presumably the courts did not or did they not care when there was no evidence, no proof?

In Jake's arms, letting go of her breath in excited little sobs, Kaye didn't feel better than anybody else and it was a new feeling.

Later that day, bruised, satisfied and rather smug, Kaye was only glad when Jake had to go to work. She went out and walked, only to turn up at his chambers in the middle of the day. The first person she encountered there was for the first time Lilian Coulthard, unmistakable, beautiful, dark, slender, and her eyes accused Kaye.

She couldn't know, Kaye thought, but she saw Kaye as competition and perhaps more. Kaye disliked her as she had always disliked Madeline and then thought perhaps it was nothing to do with either Lilian or Madeline, it was just that she would be jealous of any woman Jake loved, even now that she had been in his bed she still guarded her place. How strange, she had not realized before that she did not want anyone else there.

And she went into his room, closed the door and kissed him hard just to prove that she could. Allan would have hated her to do such a thing, at least she thought he would, she had never given them the opportunity to find out. Somehow she had regarded Allan's workplace as off limits whereas here Jake pulled her down onto his knee and kissed her.

Eighteen

Allan was surprised to receive a visit from Reggie. He was drunk, of course, it was late afternoon and Reggie always got drunk over lunch. In fact he got drunk instead of lunch, Allan thought. Mrs Semple had gone home by then and Mr Roscommon wasn't about so there was nobody to stop Reggie from making his way into Allan's room. He smiled the genial smile of the man who has been drinking steadily for several hours and is used to it.

'Allan,' he said, 'how are you?'

'I'm fine. What do you want?'

'Just wanted to tell you a morsel of gossip.'

'I'm too busy for gossip, Reg,' Allan said, frowning at the paperwork on his desk. He had had a bad enough time concentrating before Reggie came in. Now it was impossible.

'My aunt and uncle are away you know, playing golf.'

'I didn't know, strangely enough. I can't think why,' Allan said and then realized the subtleties of conversation were lost on the drunk before him.

'I'm there, of course.'

'Of course you are,' Allan said, lost as to where this was leading.

'Mind you, very often I'm not.'

'I suppose not,' Allan said and then lost patience. 'Is there a point to this, Reg?'

Reggie smirked. 'There is indeed, old boy,' he said. 'Your wife is sleeping with her cousin. He gives it to her all night. I should know, I can hear.'

Allan tried very hard not to react. His years of training came in handy.

'Should you talk about your sister like that?' was all he said.

'Aren't you surprised?' Reggie looked almost offended. 'I thought you would be.'

'She left me, as I remember. I can't say I care who she sleeps with. Now, I've got a lot of work to do. Do you mind?'

Luckily Fred came back then. Allan called him in.

'Mr Roscommon, show Mr Starr out, please. He's leaving.'

'You're very ungrateful, do you know that?' Reggie said as the door closed.

Allan would have fired something at it but Fred would have noticed. Fred noticed everything.

After that Allan had to stop himself from doing the same thing to Jake as Jake had done to him when he was sleeping with a woman he was not entitled to. Luckily he had a great deal of work to do so he didn't walk down to Old Elvet and knock Jake's teeth out. There were other ways to win.

It took Kaye by surprise when Jake's parents came back from St Andrews. She had not thought the time would pass by so quickly, she had not wanted the freedom which had been given to her during those few days and now she did not want to appear in front of Jake's mother as his . . . oh my God, what was she? His mistress? How awful. His lover? Oh dear.

To make it worse his mother cooed over her, kissed her, told her how glad they were to have her there, told her over dinner how badly Allan had treated her, how she could never go back, how she could stay with them forever. Kaye did not look at Jake across the dinner table, she did not dare. She thought he would laugh or at least let the amused look reach his eyes.

It was therefore late and the house had been silent for a long time when she slid into his room. He was working, sitting up in bed reading.

'Is this for tomorrow?'

'Yes, but I'm finished. Come here.'

She went, sat down on the bed.

'Jake—'

'Oh, don't talk to me.'

141

'Why not?'

'Because your conversation only has one subject and I'm tired of hearing about Allan and besides I know all I need to know.'

'You do?'

'I always did.'

'And what was that?'

'That you love Allan. That you'll always love him—'

'I do not. How could I?'

'Oh yes you do.'

Kaye hesitated. 'Didn't you think I loved you when I . . .'

'This is just comfort, Kaye. You've always loved me too but it's different. You can live without me. I'm not sure whether you can live without Allan. If you want him you have to fight.'

'That's beneath me.'

'No, it isn't.'

'She's young, beautiful—'

'You're Allan's wife. You're the mother of his child. He loved you for years before he saw Erin Ballantine.'

Kaye looked at him. 'This was the object of the exercise, wasn't it?'

'What?'

'That I too could . . . could go to bed with a man who isn't my husband and want him so much that I'm ashamed.'

'We were both in the same place at the same time. And you said yourself there was nothing wrong in it.' He reached for her. Kaye had promised herself she wouldn't get into this situation but it was already too late. She couldn't resist Jake.

And then she did. She pulled back out of his arms and she said to him, 'That's all it is. I mean I do love you very much but . . . If this had been the trouble between Allan and me we would have sorted it out. I want you in my arms but there's something more between Allan and me, not just Laurie but . . . I miss him.'

'Why don't you try and put it right before things go any further?'

'It's already gone too far,' Kaye said.

* * *

142

'Henry?'

Jake's father was asleep, or almost asleep, but he heard his wife's voice through long years of practice. There was no point in ignoring it, she would not be ignored. She shook his shoulder. He opened his eyes into the darkness.

'What?' he said.

'Can you hear something?'

'What kind of something?' Jake's father said, turning over.

'Jake's bedroom is at one end of the long hall, Kaye's is at the other. Somebody has just walked down between the two.'

Jake's father sighed. He had had a long day trying to sort out other people's problems. He didn't really want presenting with yet another well after midnight.

'I can't hear anything,' he said.

'What if they're sleeping together?'

'Oh, for goodness' sake. Kaye looked to me like somebody who wanted to talk. She couldn't talk to us.'

'I don't think this has much to do with talking.'

Henry sighed again.

'You didn't like Madeline, you don't like Lilian Coulthard. At least Kaye is someone you like.'

'She's married.'

'She may be divorced soon, the way things are going.'

'I can't let my son marry a divorcee, and his cousin to boot. The scandal would be incredible.'

'I don't think Jake is about to marry Kaye,' his father said tiredly.

'He may have to. What if there is a child?'

'Maude, do you think we could get some sleep? I have a lot to do tomorrow, even if you don't,' he said and turned over again.

'How can Kaye do such a thing when we have been so good to her? And how can he?'

'Maybe he's just tired of sleeping on his own. Some of us would kill for the chance,' her husband said and moments later he began to snore.

Nineteen

Diana Ballantine made a good witness for the prosecution, Allan thought with dismay. She had obviously been devoted to her brother and despised Erin and also she had convinced herself that she had seen Erin kill Angus. She sounded convincing as Jake questioned her. Yes, she had walked into the library just after the shot and there were no signs of struggle, nothing in the room had been disturbed. Lady Ballantine had the gun in her hand and was standing over her husband's body. It sounded quite conclusive.

Allan got up.

'Will you tell us about your brother's injuries, please.'

She described them and they sounded pitiful, how he had come home so badly hurt, how he had been in hospital in France for months and was then transferred to a hospital in England. She had visited him there. Then he had come home blind, lame.

'He was engaged to be married at the time, I gather.'

'He was, yes.'

'And his fiancée refused to marry him because of his injuries?'

'That's right.'

'Was he very much in love with her?'

'I believe he was.'

'Did it make him depressed?'

She considered.

'That plus the loss of any kind of life, yes, I think it did until he met Miss Marsden, as she was then.'

'There was a great discrepancy of age between them?'

'Twenty-two years.'

'Do you think it depressed him that he was married to

144

someone young and energetic and able to do all the things he couldn't do?'

'No, they were very happy.'

'In the beginning?'

She hesitated.

'Isn't it true that the marriage became less and less happy and that Lady Ballantine went home to her parents sometimes because she was distressed about her marriage?'

'I think there were difficulties, yes.'

'Is it possible that on the evening in question the difficulties had been insurmountable and your brother thought to take his own life?'

Diana Ballantine glared at him.

'No.'

'Not even possible? And that Lady Ballantine had come into the library as he did so? You don't think it could have happened?'

'No.'

'Why not?'

That stumped her for a few seconds.

'Had you ever seen her be violent towards him?'

'No.'

'Had you ever see her behave violently towards anybody?'

'No.'

'Did she know how to use a gun?'

'Not that I'm aware of.'

'But their marriage was in difficulty?'

'I think she . . . I think she found his disabilities very tiring and frustrating. I found them so myself. I think she also grew tired of the fact that there was no money, that she was obliged to go out and work and also that we had discovered we must sell the house in order to live.'

She continued. 'I think she was very upset about this and that she lost her temper. She was inordinately fond of the house, even obsessed I would say. She has never lived in a house like that before. I know she loved it.'

'A woman who has never, as far as you know, behaved violently before had a quarrel with her husband over the house and that was sufficient reason for her to want to harm him?'

145

'Yes, I think so. I think she lost her temper.'

Allan looked at Erin. She did not, he comforted himself, look like a woman who would quarrel and kill a man over a house.

'The fact remains, doesn't it, that the house will still have to be sold because there is not sufficient income to keep it going, so what could it possibly gain Lady Ballantine to kill her husband over it?'

'She could have done it in a fit of pique.'

'A fit of pique? Because of a house?' Allan said giving his voice scorn. 'I see. Thank you.'

A fortnight into the trial Jake was tired and wanted nothing more than to go home. The trouble was that his home was full of his parents, Reggie and worst of all, Kaye. He wished he had never gone to bed with Kaye. He wanted her, every night he told himself he wouldn't sleep with her and every night he did and every morning he wished that he hadn't. She was like a drug and he didn't need the distraction.

She waited for him coming home as he had no doubt she had waited so many evenings before the war for Allan, as Madeline had for him. His mother was watching them, could not have mistaken the gleam in Kaye's eyes the previous evening when he was late and they were already sitting down to dinner.

Kaye looked like a woman in love. She wore a plain black dress with pearls and all through dinner she gazed across the table at him, listened carefully to every word he said. Kaye was transparent.

His mother had come to him when he went into the study to work on the case after dinner.

'Have you considered that Mrs Coulthard might move out of your house?' she said from the doorway.

Jake looked up from where he was writing at the desk.

'What?'

'I think it might be a good idea if you moved back into your house. I love having you here, darling, but what with Reginald being so difficult and Kaye's marriage falling apart I am finding you in the middle of an important trial one problem too many. You do understand?'

146

'So I'm to move out because my cousins are causing problems?'

His mother stood for a few seconds.

'How can I put this without seeming indelicate? Kaye is becoming very fond of you.'

'Nonsense, Mother, she's always been fond of me.'

'She has left Allan. You were always the person she loved best after him. I would hate to think you became embroiled in scandalous goings on. Allan is ruining all our lives.'

Dear God, Jake thought, with some guilt, Allan's getting blamed for the whole world these days. He didn't say anything, his mother looked so tired, so concerned.

'I wish you could find some woman you really liked and marry again,' she said. 'Perhaps we should have another party—'

'I'm very busy at the moment, Mother. Let it wait.'

'I'm not sure how long things will wait,' his mother said. 'Kaye will never be able to marry again and when Erin Ballantine hangs, Allan will lose every shred of respect he ever had in this city.'

It was nice to have his mother's confidence, Jake thought, even at Allan's expense.

So the following evening he was not inclined to go home where his mother would be watching Kaye, Kaye would want to go early to bed so that she could be in his arms and Reggie would come home drunk as usual at three, singing and knocking over the hallstand. He wished he could go and see Lilian.

He was about to leave and close up the chambers when there was a knock on the outer door and someone opened it and stepped inside.

'Mr Armstrong?' the man said, pausing.

A short stocky man stood in the doorway.

'You are Mr Armstrong?'

'I am, yes. What can I do for you?'

'I've got summat to tell you.'

'Come in. Close the door.'

He hesitated for so long that Jake thought he was going to turn and run. Jake waited. He didn't say anything or move and after a while the man came inside.

'I'm Paul Halliwell. I help out at the Garden House, in the bar and . . . everything.'

'The hotel? Yes, I know it.'

'I feel like I should have come before now but . . . the thing is, Mr Armstrong, that I felt caught two ways. I wanted to say what I should but . . . I'm not even sure it's important but I can't sleep for worrying that I'm not doing the right thing.'

'Do have a seat. Anything you tell me is in confidence.'

'Yes, but if it has a bearing on the trial then you would have to do something about it?'

'If it was important, yes.'

Mr Halliwell didn't look at Jake and he didn't speak for several seconds and then he said, 'That Lady Ballantine, she has a fancy man.'

For one awful minute Jake thought that Mr Halliwell was talking about Allan and then he thought a man like that would never refer to a barrister in such a way, or would he? Jake was careful not to interrupt or ask Mr Halliwell to repeat the sentence. All he said was, as the silence went on, 'Do you know who it is?'

'Yes. He's a lad by the name of Kelvin McCormack. He lodges with her parents.'

Somewhere in Jake's memory he thought of the instinct which had never quite been listened to by his mind. He knew of the young man who lodged with them, knew that he was a pitman, that he had been their son's best friend and their son had been killed in the war and somehow Jake had known there was more to it. He cursed himself for not listening to his instincts more and he could feel the excitement. Something important was about to happen and it might win the case for him.

'Please do sit down, Mr Halliwell,' Jake said again and the man did. 'They're friends, then?' he said, inviting confidence.

'Several times they've come to the Garden House and I've given them a room. I shouldn't have but I did.'

Jake felt awful for Allan momentarily. Was this woman the kind of person who carried on relationships with two men?

'I see,' he said, trying to keep his voice level.

'The problem is . . . well, the problem isn't there any more because I know I'll lose my job coming to you like this,

148

especially if I have to go to that courtroom which I really don't want to do but I'm moving on. I wouldn't have told you else. But it seemed to me that it matters in regard of whether she did her husband in or not.'

'Yes, I should think it does. Would you be prepared to tell this to the court, it is very important?' If Mr Halliwell refused Jake was prepared to make him come to court but if he was careful here it might not come to that.

'I think I shall have to,' Mr Halliwell said.

When Kelvin answered the door at the house in Camellia Street two days later it was to a summons to appear in court. There was no point in Erin's parents not knowing since they had been in court every day, trying to support her, so he told them but fended off their questions. Perhaps he would not be asked anything which would reveal the nature of his friendship with Erin. Friendship? It made him want to kill Allan Jamieson.

The first night when Laurie came home for the Easter holidays he didn't ask questions of his mother even when she and her aunt collected him from the station and took him to her aunt and uncle's house. It was only when Kaye tucked him up in bed that he said, 'Where is Daddy?'

'He's very busy. He has a very important case.'

'Yes, I know. All about the woman who shot her husband.' Laurie said nothing more for a little while. 'Is he coming here?'

'No.'

'Are we going home?'

'No.'

And that was when he began to cry and when Kaye had finally managed to stop the tears and persuade him to talk to her he said, 'It's all my fault. I was horrid to him. I told him I wished he hadn't come home at all, that he made you cry, that I wanted not to see him again and he didn't say anything and he didn't do anything. I felt so awful afterwards because other boys' fathers would have been horrid to them and then I went back to school and I didn't get to tell him I was sorry for what I said and it's all my fault. The thing is he doesn't need to be horrid, he makes you feel awful, like he's beaten you anyway.'

He was breathless, red-faced. Kaye cuddled him to her. That was exactly how Allan made people feel, she thought.

'It was nothing to do with you,' she said. 'Daddy and I both love you very much.'

'I want to go home.'

'We can't do that.'

'I want to see Daddy. I haven't got my train set here, none of my things and I miss everything.'

He wouldn't let her go until she had promised to take him to see Allan the very next evening.

Kaye regretted it. There was no reply from the house and she had visions of Allan with Erin Ballantine, perhaps even here and not answering the door but when Laurie had insisted on going to Allan's chambers she was relieved to see that when his son burst in through the outer office and into where Allan worked that Allan was there, sitting at his desk, no doubt trying to sort out what he would be doing the next day.

Having located his father, Laurie hovered in the doorway. Allan looked surprised, pleased. His grey eyes warmed.

'Hello, old thing,' he said gently, 'how are you?'

Laurie stood like a stone.

'I want my train set,' he said.

'I think you should leave it where it is for now,' Kaye said.

'I want it. It's mine.'

'I'll send it,' Allan offered.

Laurie stared at him for a few seconds and Allan didn't pretend to himself that it boded well. There was more to this and he was going to be on the receiving end.

'Peter Hedley said that you've got another woman. I know what that means. I hate you,' Laurie said and he ran out of the room.

There was a long silence during which Kaye and Allan didn't look at one another.

'Aren't you going after him?' Allan said.

'He hasn't gone anywhere, he's just standing outside, I can see him.'

She could, her child standing on the green halfway to the

cathedral door, scrubbing at his face with his sleeve, like someone thinking of seeking sanctuary from the hideous world he finds himself in but isn't sure it will be any better once he gets past the big door. Kaye wanted to be like Laurie and hurl accusations at Allan, instead of which all she could think to utter was, 'Will you send the train set?'

'Yes, of course,' Allan said.

In the courtroom the following morning Jake stood up and said that he had two fresh witnesses. Allan got up and protested and they both went up to the judge.

'This evidence has only just come to my attention,' Jake said.

'Rubbish,' Allan said, beneath his breath.

The judge looked at him.

'It's vital to the case,' Jake said.

'I'll allow it.'

The first witness was a middle-aged man, Paul Halliwell. Allan had no idea what the connection was and could not imagine what this man could know.

'Will you tell us please, Mr Halliwell, where you first saw Lady Ballantine?' Jake said and Allan began to feel apprehensive. He made himself not look at her.

'I saw her the day that she came to the Garden House Hotel with Kelvin McCormack. I was working there at the time and he had worked with me and we'd been friends.'

'She came there with him?'

'Yes.'

'In what capacity?'

'They wanted a room.'

A murmur went through the court.

'For the night?'

'No, not all of it.'

'They spent several hours there?'

'They did, yes.'

'Was that the only time you saw Lady Ballantine there?'

'No, it happened a lot. I would sneak them into whichever room wasn't being used. Nobody knew and it meant they didn't have to pay,' Mr Halliwell said.

The second witness was a young man in a cheap suit. Jake

151

had been right, he was dragging his feet as though he wanted to run away much as Laurie had run away the previous evening. Allan had found it very difficult to concentrate after that. He hadn't realized the gossip had got down to the level of small boys but the whole place was talking about the case so perhaps it was not surprising.

The stupid part was that he had wanted to run to Erin, whereas in fact they were spending very little time together, firstly because he didn't think it was right for them to be seen out together socially, secondly he didn't want her out anywhere because he thought it might hinder their case and thirdly from a purely practical viewpoint they had nowhere to go. He couldn't take her to his house, she had not come to chambers since long before the trial began and she was staying with her parents, in a tiny little pit cottage, and there was no earthly chance he could go there without being seen and without causing further gossip though it sounded to him as though things were about as bad as they could get.

He had gone home and taken refuge in the garden. It was late spring and everything was coming into bloom. On the banksides the last of the daffodils and narcissi still lingered. The pansies were cream, lilac and black, the French lavender was tall and bright. There was angelica with its long fluffy pink flowers, heathers here and there in white, purple and pale lilac. Daisies covered the grass in big groups.

As he wandered, and the wind turned cold and the light began to go from what had been a grey evening, a squirrel ran through the grass before him and a pigeon beat its wings just further over. There were big swathes of bluebells and pink campion under the trees, magpies and blackbirds. Rabbits scuttled into the undergrowth as he walked down the hill away from the house.

The smell of honeysuckle wafted towards him in the slight breeze. All the trees had on them bright new leaves except for the foxglove tree, which had no flowers or leaves, only tiny buds, hardly discernible. It was at the very limit of its natural surroundings. A chilly season, a sunless summer and mist and it would be lucky to survive. Who had brought it here, Allan wondered, to struggle in the cold north winds?

152

He went back inside and sat over a log fire, taking comfort from that and tried not to think about Laurie. He had to concentrate. He could not let Erin suffer because of such distractions.

The young man took the stand and Allan had that feeling, the feeling of doom as Jake questioned him. He glanced at Erin and she sat there like a petrified rabbit. He just hoped none of the jury were watching her face. And then the nightmare began.

'Will you tell us please your relationship to the accused?'

The boy looked blankly at him.

'I lodged with her parents.'

'Mr McCormack, you are under oath. What is your relationship to the defendant?'

'We were friends.'

'What kind of friends?'

'Good friends.'

'Mr McCormack, did you on more than one occasion take Lady Ballantine to the Garden House Hotel in the north end of the city?'

Kelvin McCormack's eyes were full of panic.

He didn't answer.

'I'll change the question. How many times did you take Lady Ballantine to the Garden House Hotel?'

Kelvin McCormack hesitated.

'I don't remember.'

'You don't remember?' Jake consulted the papers in front of him. 'Do you want me to refresh your memory?'

'We went there several times.'

There was silence which Jake deliberately allowed to lengthen, Allan thought.

'You hired a room?'

'Sort of.'

'Do you mean "unofficially"?'

'Yes. I had an arrangement with a man who works there.'

'So, I'll ask you again, Mr McCormack. What was your relationship with the defendant?'

'I was her . . .' It seemed to Allan that the young man cast a triumphant look at him. 'We were lovers.'

The sound in the court was deafening, it seemed to Allan.

153

'And this was after she was married?'

'Until very recently.'

'You spent a lot of time with her?'

'She was unhappy. We . . .' The young man had the grace to falter.

Oh God, Allan thought.

'What did she tell you about her marriage?'

'She said she wished that she had never married him. She hated him. We planned to run away. She was going to marry me until she met him. She liked him for his big house, his title and his money. I don't blame her for that, I understand how it happened but she had promised to marry me and then she wrote to me and told me she'd met a gentleman. That was the way she put it, a gentleman.'

Sensing Erin was about to speak Allan shook his head very slightly. The colour had gone from her face and her eyes were almost black with tears and worry.

'Was she going to tell her husband you were planning to run away?'

'Yes. The – the night that . . . he died but she said that he would never let her go, that she didn't want to tell him.'

'And did she say that she had told him?'

'Yes.'

'And how did she say he reacted?'

'He was angry. He didn't want her to leave.'

'She was going to leave him because she loved you?'

'I thought she did at the time.' The young man's voice was soft with shame and want, Allan thought, and slight grievance too. He threw a resentful glance in Allan's direction.

'She would gain everything if she murdered him?' Jake said. 'Isn't that so?'

'I don't know what you mean.'

'Yes, you do. The house, her freedom and the man she loved. That is why you've kept quiet about this, isn't it?'

'She asked me not to say anything. She said it would finish her if they found out.' He looked wildly at Jake. 'I love her. I always loved her. I would have done anything for her.'

'Would you have killed, Mr McCormack?'

There was silence. Allan made himself not object, as he

154

had made himself do several times during this testimony. It would only have made things worse, drawn further attention to a damaging situation.

'Thank you. That's all,' Jake said.

The judge looked at Allan.

'Do you have any questions for this witness, Mr Jamieson?'

'No, my lord.'

When the afternoon finally drew to a close all Allan wanted was to go home. He made himself not hurry away, he made himself not draw away from Erin. They walked out of the courthouse together and then he turned around the corner into the quiet place where he had parked his car. She followed him there.

'Go back to your parents,' was all he said.

'Allan, I'm sorry.'

'Just go.'

'I want us to talk about this.'

'No.' He would have got into the car and driven away but she got in with him so he drove faster than he had ever driven across the small city before. It was just as well it wasn't far, around the corner, up New Elvet towards the outskirts of the city and then past the New Inn and out on the road to Darlington.

There, on the left, lay his house, the place he wanted to be, and now that the final thing seemed to have gone wrong in his life, he wanted to be there alone. He turned in and up the hill and usually he would look left because it was such a wonderful view of the cathedral when you got up there but today he turned right and into the drive and stopped behind the house. He tried to leave her there but she got hold of his arm.

'Allan, please.'

And then Allan lost his temper, as he had not done when Laurie had shouted at him, or when Kaye had left him. He got hold of her and shook her.

'You stupid girl. You stupid, stupid girl. How could you lie to me? Do you know what this is going to do to our case? It's finished, it's over.' He wrenched away. Erin stood there, sobbing. 'What on earth were you doing, going to bed with Kelvin McCormack, and why in hell didn't you tell me? Don't you know that for a woman in this country adultery is as bad as murder? And then you went to bed with me. God knows why—'

'You didn't complain!'

'I didn't know it was just so that I would help you. You didn't have to do that. I would have done the best for you anyway. Is this what men are to you? They have to be . . . manoeuvred around, got on your side and you would go so far as to bed them for reasons other than because you want them? Well? You made use of that poor bastard and then you did the same with me. Don't you think anybody is ever going to help you without you drop your knickers for them first?'

'I love you.'

'No.'

He didn't listen to her even though she pleaded and cried. He took from the car his briefcase and his papers though he didn't know why because he said, 'You can get yourself some other idiot, I'm done with this.'

'Allan, you can't.' She can after him. 'You can't leave me. They'll hang me, you know they will.'

'I don't care any more.'

He tried to get into the house without her and God alone knew what the servants would think when she followed him in, screaming and crying. He bundled her into the nearest room and closed the door on them.

'Shut up,' he said. He couldn't stop the anger, the idea that she had slept with Kelvin McCormack as well as him.

'I didn't kill him,' she said, crying. 'You have to believe me. I didn't. Kelvin was nice to me, he's a nice man, a decent man. I needed . . . I needed somebody other than a man who couldn't see, who couldn't walk—'

'Who couldn't perform in bed? That's the point, isn't it? He couldn't do it.'

Into the silence which followed she said, 'I'm twenty. I couldn't bear it. I didn't understand when I married him how awful it was going to be. You have no idea how horrible it was being in bed with him and him . . .'

'So you killed him.'

'I did not kill him. And it wasn't just that. You make me sound shallow and mean and I'm not. I just knew that if I told you about Kelvin, if it got out, that I wouldn't come out of this alive.'

She stood before the fire and Allan went over and watched the rain pour down the windows.

'There's no way back out of this. You've lost any credibility you might have had. If you'd been a man it would have been bad enough but the odds are stacked against a woman even more so.'

In the garden the rain had turned the rhododendrons to pink, orange and red smudges, the peonies yellow and red, almost as big as his hand and further over white lilac, primulas with huge pink flowers like bells and hydrangeas with big pink hanging heads.

Further over he could see the conservatories to one side and then further down in his imagination he could see the ponds and the little waterfalls so lovingly constructed by his godmother, slate and stone, the water running all over, darkening everything in its path.

'You should have trusted me,' Allan said.

'I don't want to die,' she said and when he turned around she had her arms clasped around herself for comfort and her head was down.

'Did you really think I wouldn't help you if you didn't let me bed you?'

She looked up. Her eyes were drenched.

'It wasn't like that. I'd never met anybody like you before and I was so afraid. Please, Allan—'

'I'm not going to go on with this case. You can't expect it and nobody else will. I'm going to the judge to tell him so—'

'You can't. Even if you hate me, you'll never have another peaceful moment if I die.'

Allan laughed. 'You think I sleep peacefully now? You're just another person I defended. I have to lose some time. The fact that I slept with you isn't good obviously but I can forgive myself anything. I've killed people too, you see. Once you've killed there is nowhere to go. Numbers don't matter. I've blown men's heads away. You're nothing to me.'

'You told me that no matter how bad things got I was to trust you.'

'You told me that you wouldn't lie to me.'

'Please, don't do this to me.'

'Get out of my sight.'

She stared at him for a few seconds and then she ran.

By the time Jake got home it was obvious to him that Kaye had been told exactly what had happened. Her uncle would know, her aunt would know by now.

'He's finished here, isn't he?' she guessed.

'Yes, I would say he'd burned his boats,' Jake said lightly when he was feeling anything but. He had not realized he would feel betrayal, guilt, remember in horrible detail the day that Allan had saved his life in Flanders. There was nothing left between him and Allan now. He had bedded Allan's wife and beaten him in open court, so personally and professionally Allan was on the floor. If he had been a boxer they would have counted him out.

'Do you think she'll hang?'

'Almost certainly,' Jake said.

'Then Allan will have nobody.'

Jake looked at her but he didn't say anything.

'My uncle has recommended me a divorce solicitor. I'm seeing him tomorrow,' she said. 'When all this comes out Allan won't stand a chance. I'm so worried about him, Jake. Isn't that stupid?'

When Erin finally got home it was late and dark and nobody spoke. Her father didn't even get up, her mother had obviously been crying.

'I'm so sorry,' Erin said, closing the back door and venturing down the one step between pantry and kitchen. 'I didn't mean for any of this to happen.'

'We thought when our John was killed that things couldn't get any worse,' her mother said. 'Then when they accused you of killing your husband we thought things couldn't get any worse. We thought you hadn't done it. We thought you were still respectable but for you and Kelvin to carry on like that . . .'

'Mr Jamieson has said he won't represent me any more.

158

He says it's finished and if he won't look after me then there's nothing I can do, even if they can get somebody else to help. I'm going to die because of what I've done, not because of Angus but because of Kelvin.'

Her father finally looked at her.

'We've stood by you this long,' he said, 'we'll go on standing by you. There's nothing else to do. Why don't you go to bed? We have another day to face tomorrow though how we shall get through it I have no idea.'

Late in the evening Mrs Mackenzie came softly into the study where Allan was sitting with his back to his desk, staring out at the night.

'I want to have a word with you, Mr Jamieson, that is if you don't mind.'

'Sit down,' Allan said. 'You're not leaving, are you, because of what's happened?'

She looked shocked even as she sat down across the desk.

'Never in this world,' she said and made him smile. 'It's about something quite different. It seems to me that you should be told. Mary's Joe . . . you were good to him and he . . . he knew Sir Angus Ballantine's man that used to chauffeur for him. He wasn't a proper chauffeur like your dad used to have, just somebody to make them look good, they could hardly afford to pay him.' Mrs Mackenzie sniffed.

Allan waited.

'But he knew about the goings on at the house and that Sir Angus had tried to do himself in.'

Allan stared at her.

'He did?'

'Aye, he did. The chauffeur was involved once and the sister she was upset and she told him that when they pulled Sir Angus out of the lake it was not the first time he'd tried. She'd taken pills away from him as well.'

'And the other time?'

'Tried to shoot himself,' Mrs Mackenzie said in triumph. 'I told Joe he should have come to you and told you before but he didn't like to, seeing as it's just the chauffeur's word, isn't it?'

'Was there no doctor called when Sir Angus did these things?'

Mrs Mackenzie looked hard at him.

'I never thought about that,' she said.

Later still, Allan had a visitor. Mrs Mackenzie came into the room once more.

'Mr Armstrong is here, sir, I put him in the library.'

He went through to find Jake fidgeting before the fire.

'Should you be here?'

'I didn't know about Kelvin McCormack,' Jake said. 'Honestly, Allan, I didn't know before.'

'It's all right,' Allan said.

Jake looked at him.

'You always said that in France.'

'I was right, wasn't I?'

'Without fail.'

'Well, then.'

Jake faltered.

'You were there for me.'

'Don't do this to yourself,' Allan advised him.

'You were. I wished you weren't sometimes, I just wanted to die after Madeline . . .'

'I know.'

'My life is so – so very small and I . . .'

'It's your job to do your best, I haven't taken it personally.'

'There's more.'

'I know there is.'

'You do?'

'Of course I do. Reggie came to see me.'

'Oh God, Allan, I'm sorry—'

'It was finished before you got there. You didn't take anything from me, it was long gone. Kaye and I . . . were finished, it was over. Don't worry about it, Jake, it doesn't matter.' It wasn't true of course, it would never be true. His wife, the person he had loved so very much, had gone to bed with her cousin, his best friend, a man Allan had shielded so very often in France. She wouldn't sleep with him but she would sleep with Jake. Allan understood, at least in part. She was taking revenge for Erin Ballantine and Jake was lost, lonely. Who else would she go to, but it hurt so very much, though he would never admit that to Jake or let him know how very angry he was.

'How can you say that when things are in such a mess? Your marriage is . . . she's talking about going to a solicitor, divorcing you. She'll get it on grounds of adultery. I didn't intend it to be like this.'

'I know.'

'You know too bloody much,' Jake said. 'It isn't respectable for people to know so much.'

'Do you want a drink?'

Jake hesitated.

Allan went over and poured whisky from the decanter for them.

'Sit down,' he urged.

'You're going to sit me down and then strangle me,' Jake said.

'Sit down. And stop worrying about things. You can't support both sides at once.'

They sat down. They drank.

'Kaye is seeing Edgar Blair tomorrow.'

Allan said nothing.

'He's a shit,' Jake said.

'He's also the best. I presume you recommended him.'

'My father did.'

'Oh, right.'

'Will you fight for your boy?'

Allan looked down into his drink.

'No, I can't do that to Kaye. Laurie is her whole life.'

'What will you do after the trial?'

Allan sighed and sat further back and took another sip of whisky.

'I don't know. Sell up and leave, I suppose. What else is there to do?'

'What about the house and the gardens?'

'Kaye could live here.'

'I don't imagine she wants to.'

161

'No, probably not.'

'What will you do?'

'Take Erin away.'

Jake stared at him. Allan wished he could hold that look in his memory, the surprise. It was his first moment of triumph over Jake.

'But . . . Allan . . . You're going to lose.'

Allan smiled.

'You think so?' he said.

'What more is there?'

'Haven't you ever heard the phrase "it isn't over till it's over"?'

'But it is over.'

'Oh, Jake . . .'

Jake heard that in his sleep. He told himself again and again that he had won, that Allan could have nothing left, he had nowhere to go. Jake was reminded of Allan's voice in his troubled dreams, the slow smile, the idle way he said Jake's name and he was back in France and Allan was assuring him it would be all right, only Jake knew that somebody was going to get his head blown off. He only hoped it wouldn't be him.

Mrs Mackenzie, Allan thought, as he went to bed, would not have given him up for anything. If he went anywhere he would obliged to take her with him and the other servants too because all of them were people he had helped. Mrs Mackenzie's husband had killed another man in a drunken brawl but Allan had got him off. He had died within the year but it was a year they would not have had.

The kitchen maid, Mary, her man was a poacher and Allan had got him off too and they had been married. He was the gardener now and kept the place right. And Fiona was just married and Allan had taken him on too. She had been a thief and there was nothing better than a thief reformed for looking after your property and her husband had been a drunk and homeless. They had a house in the grounds. And now it was Erin's turn and everything would be all right.

Twenty

Kaye had imagined that going through with this would be a lot easier than it actually was. To tell somebody else, somebody she didn't know, about her failed marriage was humiliating and however kind and sympathetic Mr Blair was it was insufficient to help.

'You should not have left the marital home,' he said.

'What?'

'You shouldn't have walked out. It's a lot more difficult to claim part of it when you aren't there.'

'I don't want it,' Kaye said.

'Mrs Jamieson, if I may be so bold, you must learn to be practical. Your husband is worth a great deal of money and you are entitled to a lot of it. It is a well-known fact that he has committed adultery and with a woman who . . . well, let us not discuss that – we will find evidence later, I have no doubt.'

It occurred to Kaye that Mr Blair's feelings for Allan went beyond the professional. He didn't like him. This was presumably one of the problems of having a husband in the legal business. You were bound to find people who disliked him, envied him. Allan was rich and clever, young and it had to be said, six inches taller than Mr Blair and perhaps it mattered to Mr Blair to try and better Allan. He seemed to be taking a great deal of satisfaction from it.

'You are the injured party.'

The injured party. Kaye's mind was filled with Allan coming home from France grey-faced, exhausted, defiant, sleepless, taking no comfort from anything, spending hours in the garden. She had hated him being away, she had hated him coming home somebody different whom she scarcely recognized. He didn't talk about the war, she didn't ask.

Most of all she hated how Allan suffered because his health had always been precarious and she became increasingly angry as time went on and he took everything personally, doing more and more for his men, caring about each one who was hurt or killed and when he came home there was nothing left to give herself and Laurie. Allan was sucked dry by the war.

Other people had come to her in the street, telling her what good care Lieutenant Colonel Jamieson had taken of her husband, her brother, her son, how kind, how caring he had been, doing everything he could and after Allan got the VC, something else they didn't talk about, when he had held some stupid piece of ground against all comers, other women stopped her in the street and told her what a hero he was.

Oh yes, Kaye thought, Allan was a hero to other people. To her he was the man who cried out until she could not sleep in the same room, who could not speak for fear of saying the wrong thing, who had no interest in her beyond sex, who did not even enquire for his son. Allan could hardly see or hear when he came home. She was glad when he did not.

She had lost Allan a long time ago. The trouble was she had not realized you could lose people over and over again in so many different ways that it seemed never ending. The only thing was to cut loose for good and never to see them again and even then, even years and years away, she would lose Allan over and over because once you had loved someone it was the one thing you had left when it was all finished.

Twenty-One

The look of relief on Erin's face when he appeared made Allan feel guilty and small but he gave her a reassuring smile and then he went to her and pressed her hand and whispered, 'Don't worry.'

He gave instructions to Mr Roscommon that he was to keep Diana Ballantine and their doctor away from one another, in separate rooms outside the court if need be until they were called into the court to give evidence. He did not want Diana Ballantine to know that Dr Calland was to be questioned first. If Mrs Mackenzie was to be believed Diana Ballantine's evidence would differ considerably.

Dr Calland was a small meek-looking man, balding, tired, the kind of man who is about to retire and is only glad of it.

'You attended Sir Angus Ballantine at his home on a number of occasions after he was badly injured in France and came home?' Allan said.

'I did, yes.'

'I gather that upon one of these occasions you were called there in the middle of the night. It was January, nineteen sixteen. Can you tell us what had happened?'

The doctor did not look happy to be there and mumbled something.

'Can you speak up, please?'

'Sir Angus attempted suicide.' Dr Calland looked at Allan as much as to say, 'As you so obviously very well know.'

The courtroom was no longer silent but when the noise had died down Dr Calland said, 'It was a very long time ago. He was ill. He had just come home.'

'How did he do this?'

'He tried to shoot himself.'

It seemed to Allan at that point that the court exploded like a firework and he had never been happier to hear any sound.

'His sister, Diana, saved him. She came into the room and wrestled the gun from his hands. He's a very big man but he was disabled and blind and . . . very upset.'

'Isn't it true, Dr Calland, that Angus Ballantine tried to kill himself on more than one occasion?'

The doctor hesitated and then said, 'He was extremely depressed.'

'Is that "yes"?'

'Yes.'

'He did try to kill himself more than once?'

'Yes.'

'How many times?'

'Three.'

'The third attempt was in fact just prior to his meeting his wife?'

'Yes.'

'Lady Ballantine therefore knew nothing of this?'

'As far as I am aware. Unless he or his sister told her.'

'Thank you, Dr Calland,' Allan said and sat down.

Jake got up. He said, 'Isn't it the case, Dr Calland, that Sir Angus was no longer depressed after his marriage and that in fact he made no further suicide attempt?'

'As far as I am aware that is true.'

Allan got up again.

'You examined the body. Is it possible that Sir Angus committed suicide?'

'Yes, I suppose it's possible. He had a history of depression and his body was failing him in a good many ways.'

'Will you elaborate?'

'His sight was totally gone, the lameness was getting worse. It's my belief he would soon have become an invalid. The stresses and strains of war had worn him out at a young age.'

'Was he capable of physical contact in marriage?'

'I believe not,' Dr Calland said.

'Could this have depressed him further?'

'It could have done, yes.'

166

When Allan sat down it took all his strength not to throw a triumphant glance at Jake.

Diana Ballantine resembled a cross hen when she was recalled, he thought. He barely gave her time to settle into her chair before he said, 'You came upon Lady Ballantine on the evening that your brother died. Will you tell us exactly what you saw?'

'I opened the library door just as she killed him.'

'Remember that you are under oath, Miss Ballantine.'

'I saw her shoot him. She hated him. She wanted rid of him. He had decided to sell the house. She only married him to get the house. And all the time they were married she was committing adultery with that – that pitboy. She was deceitful. She lied her way into that marriage and she killed my brother to get out of it and take the house.'

'Tell me, Miss Ballantine, is it possible that you are mistaken and that your brother took his own life, that Lady Ballantine came upon him doing so?'

'They were shouting. I could hear them from the hall. There was never any question of him doing such a thing.'

'Had he ever attempted to take his life?'

'Certainly not.'

The room was so silent that when somebody coughed it echoed.

'He never tried to kill himself?'

'She killed him. I told you.'

Allan let several seconds go by and then he said, 'Dr Calland testified that your brother tried to take his life upon three separate occasions. Are you telling us he is mistaken or a liar?'

She didn't answer.

'Isn't it the truth, Miss Ballantine, that you only came into the room because you heard a shot and that you had just seen Lady Ballantine run into the room because she too had heard it and that your brother, finding his marriage was nothing more than a sham, that he had turned an innocent young woman's head by pretending to her that he could provide her with some kind of fairy tale and made her life and thereby his own life a misery, decided to take the decent way out and end it?'

'It's not true. She killed him.'

167

'He never attempted suicide, ever?'

Diana Ballantine began to weep.

'He didn't mean it,' she said. 'That fiancée of his, she wouldn't have him any more and Erin Marsden was nothing more than a common pitman's daughter.'

'The fact is that you hate her, don't you?'

'I hate everything she did to him.'

'You hate her so much that you wanted to believe that she had killed him? Isn't that right?'

'She's a gold-digger, a money-grabber, she never cared about him.'

'He took his own life, as he had tried to do so often before, didn't he?'

'No. He never did. That doctor is a liar. Angus was a fine upstanding man, kind and generous and intelligent—'

'Generous enough to give his wife her freedom when he had nothing else left to offer her?'

'No. She did it. She drove him to it.'

'She drove him to kill himself. Isn't that what you mean?'

Diana Ballantine was weeping openly.

'Didn't you save him three times by attending him very closely, by staying his hand when he would have shot himself, by pulling him out of the lake in the grounds, by throwing away pills by which he could have damaged himself even more and didn't his wife attempt to do exactly the same thing on the night that he died?'

She didn't answer.

'Didn't he, Miss Ballantine?'

'I don't know.'

'You don't know? You didn't see Lady Ballantine do anything more than run into that room after she heard a shot. Isn't that right?'

Diana Ballantine sat with her head down. The judge leaned over towards her.

'You must answer the question, Miss Ballantine.'

She raised her head.

'The truth is that Angus had nothing more to live for and it was all her fault. He married her. I didn't want him to but he was lonely and tired and the war had taken everything from us. We had nothing left. She was the only light in Angus's life, that common little trollop. She married him because of who he was, she never cared about him, never.'

'He killed himself, didn't he, Miss Ballantine?'

'He wanted to die, yes. Why would he not? Why would anybody not in such circumstances?'

As they sat, waiting for the verdict, Allan did not look at Erin. The jurors were all men and he was still doubtful since he did not think it had been made completely clear. Would they be able to see that the issue was still clouded, would always be clouded? All he had tried to do was lead Diana Ballantine to say that she saw – what? Something she didn't see. What had she seen? Only Erin knew that. Everybody else was guessing and he had led them away from the idea and it was as much as he could do.

When they came back he panicked inside himself. He did not think that Erin deserved to die even if she had killed her husband. Marriages were impossible things even between the most well-meaning people, what would it be like in a union where the two people had nothing in common at all and had made one another miserable?

The verdict was delivered and it was 'not guilty'. Allan felt the stone roll off his back and somehow it was not just the weight of the trial but all the difficulties of his life. He remembered the man that he had been before the war, he remembered what being happy was like and where his place was in the world.

The only reaction from Erin was that she stood with her head down in a kind of disbelief. Later when he had her to himself in a tiny room beside the court she threw herself into his arms.

'Oh, Allan, thank you so much. I don't think you have any idea how I feel.'

He did and he knew that it would not last. Once she got used to the idea that she had been cleared and had her freedom what was she to do with her life?

Her mother and father took her home. They were right to do so, he thought, she was not ready to go back to Broke Hall. He wasn't sure that she ever would be.

Twenty-Two

Jake thought about going to see Lilian. He wanted to move out of his parents' house for so many reasons that he could hardly sleep or breathe while he was there but since he didn't know how to suggest to her that he wanted to live there he was almost relieved when Lilian came to him in the office late that afternoon when she had finished work and suggested the same thing.

'You've found somewhere else?'

'Yes.'

She wasn't friendly, Jake surmised, looking across the desk at her. He couldn't understand why that was. Lilian was hardly the kind of woman who cared whether he lost or won his cases. You couldn't win everything. Was it something else?

'A nice house?'

'I expect it will do,' she said. 'I've imposed long enough. I can't thank you for what you've done for me. I know that it . . . went against your better judgement—'

'No, it didn't,' Jake said instantly and she looked at him and then he thought she smiled in spite of herself. 'That was my better judgement, Lilian.' He didn't often call her by her first name, in fact she didn't think he ever had done before, and it seemed to alter the whole of the relationship between them so that he said with a hungry look on his face, 'How's Nora?'

'She's very well. I'm sorry you lost the case.'

'Oh, it's only work,' he said lightly when he didn't feel light.

He had hated losing. He had especially hated losing to Allan. Allan was not the man to gloat but lots of people had come to him in the court and shaken his hand and smiled and offered him their warmest congratulations. Jake felt somehow as though he had lost for himself, for Kaye and that he still had the right of it. His instincts told him that Erin Ballantine had cared nothing for her husband and everything for her house and she had won. 'Where is your new place?'

'It's further out of town.'

'Oh? Nice area?'

'It'll be fine.'

'Maybe I could . . . maybe I could . . .'

'I don't think so,' she said before he got any further.

'I don't know what to say.'

'There isn't much you can say but I'll always be grateful to you—'

'That sounds final.'

'I've got another job.' She didn't say, 'I couldn't work near you any more considering what's happened,' but Jake heard it anyhow.

'Where?'

Lilian shook her head.

'You've been . . . you've been nicer to me than anybody else ever was. I—'

Jake got up and came around the desk to her and Lilian backed into the door.

'No,' she said. 'This is how it's supposed to be.'

Jake looked hard at her.

'Why?' he said.

She didn't answer immediately and then she said, 'I work with you and . . . I saw when Mrs Jamieson came to the office.'

'Lilian—'

'I must go. I have a lot to do. I finish here on Friday,' and Lilian hauled open the door and hurried away.

Kaye had not been able to rest at all that day and wished she had gone to court and kept changing her mind so when she heard the door she ran out of the library and her uncle stood there in the hall and the look on his face told her what had happened.

'Allan won?'

'He did.'

Kaye had told herself she would be sorry if it happened but she wasn't. There was a part of her which was proud of him just as she was always proud of his abilities. She wasn't even sorry for Jake. To Jake it had been a trial. To Allan it had been everything. What would he do now? Would he run away with Erin Ballantine? Would Allan leave his beloved house for her?

People were talking, it was true but they would talk about him differently now that he had got her off. He could marry Erin Ballantine if he chose and go to live with her there. He had enough money to buy half a dozen beautiful houses and he would be able to keep her well and in time Kaye thought, they would probably have children and she would be left, she and Laurie would be forgotten.

Her aunt was most upset for Jake and even more so because of Kaye. She cried though she tried not to. When Jake got home they had a very quiet dinner except for Reggie who sneered, 'Good old Jake. Shame about that.'

Normally, Kaye thought, Jake would have cared, replied, taken Reggie on but he didn't, he just ate his dinner and left the dining room as soon as was polite. Kaye followed him out.

'Where are you going?'

'The pub.'

'I want to talk to you.'

'Not now, please.' Jake paused with one hand on the outside door and said with a short smile, 'I have had a spectacularly bad day.'

'What do you think will happen?'

'Shouldn't you talk to Allan about that? And by the way, I'm moving back into my house next week. Lilian has found somewhere else to live and another job.'

'You're moving out? What about me?'

Jake glanced at the dining-room door in case his parents should overhear. He didn't say anything. Kaye came to him.

'You can't leave me here.'

'What do you suggest I do? You can't move in with me and my parents have told me they want rid of me.'

172

'They want you to go?'

'Of course they do. They aren't stupid. They know what's going on.'

This had not occurred to her though she thought of late that Jake's mother's attitude towards her had changed to something that resembled wood but she had put that down to the trial and her position as Allan's estranged wife.

'Do you realize that if you leave me here and I divorce Allan I could be living with your parents forever?'

'There'll be a settlement, you'll have your own place—'

'You think I want to live alone? Why don't you just be honest for once in your miserable life and admit that you're tired of me?'

'It's not that,' he said, 'I love Lilian.'

'You love Lilian Coulthard?'

'Yes, I do.'

'That didn't stop you sleeping with me.'

'I'm sorry. You could be honest too and admit that you're never going to love anyone like you loved Allan,' Jake said and he walked out.

For seconds after he had gone Kaye wanted to cry, call him names, run after him and do what? She didn't know and then she was angry with him, with Allan but mostly with herself, and she had an overwhelming desire to go home.

Moving back into his own house was almost as bad as Jake had thought it would be. It was a house without Madeline and it was also now a house without Lilian Coulthard and the lovely little girl he had come to care for. There was no evidence, he thought, that any woman had ever lived there. It was cool, silent and seemed to him so ghastly that he immediately went off to the pub and stayed there until very late at night.

His mother had told him that she would find him someone to do the cleaning. 'You ought to have several servants,' she said.

'In a house that size?'

'You're a single man. You cannot afford to have just one live-in maid. It's bad form.'

A single man. What an awful way to be referred to, Jake thought. His mother was pleased with him, looked approvingly at him and kept inviting him to dinner parties just as Kaye had and always with the same idea in mind. That he would marry again. Kaye barely spoke to him any more and Jake could think of nothing to say to any of the women he was introduced to.

They were all lovely but they were not Lilian. Eventually he found his courage to search for her and asked around among his associates and discovered that Lilian was working for a solicitor in Chester-le-Street and living there too. Jake discovered the address and on the next Saturday morning he motored out there.

It was not in Chester-le-Street, it was one of the little pit villages around, and when he finally discovered her new abode it was a tiny house in a terrace in a back street. Jake left his car at some distance and walked but when he had banged on the door and she opened it with the child in her arms he was so pleased he had gone there even though Lilian looked anything but glad to see him.

'You'd better come in,' she said as though it was a last resort.

Jake went in and it was as unlike his house when she had lived in it as anything could be. He had not thought how badly Lilian would be paid for what she did, that she would have to pay somebody to see to Nora when she was at work and that she would have very little money left after that for food and clothing.

The furniture was old and scarred and Lilian had obviously been cleaning the dark little hall because there was a bucket and mop and it was wet and she was flustered, the little curls of hair sticking to her moist brow. Nora didn't seem to recognize him.

She took him into the kitchen and the sunshine came in through the window which looked out over the back yard.

'I didn't expect you to come here,' she said putting down the child, who sat and played with her toys. Jake couldn't help watching Nora and wishing she would come to him so that he could pick her up and hold her in his arms. As for her mother, he couldn't even look at Lilian.

'Or want me to?'

'Or that either. You cannot stay. My neighbours will see you.'

'Lilian, please.' He finally did look at her only to find a dismissive gaze on her face and something more which he could not discern. Nora had come back to her mother, sensing perhaps that there was something wrong. Lilian picked her up.

'Oh, don't,' she said. 'It was never going to amount to anything and now it definitely isn't. You're not the person I thought you were and . . . I'm sure you think I should be grateful for your attentions but—'

'Oh God, I don't,' Jake said.

'I was grateful for everything you did for us. I know that without you we probably wouldn't be here but it has to stop somewhere, the gratitude and it stopped for me . . .'

'When Kaye came to my office.'

'Mrs Jamieson, yes.' Jake would have said something but Lilian didn't give him time. She said. 'There's no point in telling me that you aren't having an affair with her because I could tell just by looking at her. She didn't have to come to the office and . . . throw herself at you like that.

'I know that well-off people carry on like that and I'm sure you think it's all right but I . . . That's the difference, you see. Men like you they think they can have anything and that anything becomes them. I've never been in a position to behave like that.'

She shifted the child in her arms and finally put Nora down and the little girl hid among her skirts. 'I sound awful, I know I do, I didn't mean to but . . . I couldn't bear it if a man I cared about went to bed with somebody else and how would you ever trust him again?'

Jake couldn't imagine. In fact he couldn't imagine anything any more and was reduced to watching the little girl and thinking how beautiful she was with her fair skin and black hair and dark eyes and perfect little hands which now clutched at Lilian's dress.

'I think that you had better go.'

Jake thought so too. He couldn't bear a second longer and

by the time he had walked down the street and got into his car he couldn't see to drive and was obliged to sit there, to the great interest of everybody who went past, until his vision had cleared and then he went back to Durham.

There, somehow, in the house where Madeline and his child had died, he sat down and cried for the first time, for Madeline and the baby and for Lilian and Nora but also for himself and afterwards knew that he was no longer confusing them. He loved Lilian Coulthard, he would have loved her even if he had never met Madeline, even if she had not had such an entrancing little girl. He wanted to marry her, he didn't think he could manage another minute without her but he would have to. There was nothing more he could do.

Twenty-Three

It was half-past four in the afternoon and it was raining. Erin had dreamed of sitting over the fire in her house, eating toast and drinking tea, had thought of it so much during the trial. Now it was hers. She had gone back to Lilac Street to visit her parents to find that Kelvin had moved back in.

The horrid little terraced house looked so dear to her now, she loved the way that the fire burned in the kitchen and the brass which her mother polished each week glowed against the shiny black of the fireplace.

She loved the smell of her mother's brilliant cooking, she was making pot pie, a suet crust and beneath it potatoes, onions and beef in rich gravy. She longed to accept her mother's invitation to stay for a meal but she didn't feel as if she could, she felt as though she had betrayed and hurt her parents to the extent where she could not stay with them any more. They looked so old, they had gone through so much and she had caused a great deal of it.

They tactfully left Kelvin and Erin alone in the front room. From there she could hear the sound of children playing ball games outside and remembered what it had been like when they were small and she wished to be a child and to begin again and to have nothing to worry about and to play outside in the fading light knowing that the lights were burning in the little house for when she was weary enough to cease her game and seek the shelter of her family's love.

'I miss John.'

She hadn't meant to say it.

'Aye, I miss him too. Erin, look, I'm sorry for what happened. They made me come to court. I wouldn't have done it otherwise. I never meant you any harm. I was jealous

177

of Mr Jamieson, I admit it. I would be Allan Jamieson if I could.'

Erin was so ashamed she couldn't think of anything to say.

'I went with him on purpose, I think,' she managed and then wanted to bite out her tongue that she had said something so terrible.

'You couldn't have done.'

'That's how it seems now and I'm sure he thinks so. I would have done anything to get him to save me.'

'But you must've known he would do his best anyway.'

'Perhaps.'

'Are you going to marry him?'

'I don't know. He hasn't said anything. I don't like his son. Isn't that awful?'

'I suppose it's understandable. I want you to be happy, Erin. If he makes you happy—'

'He doesn't. He isn't in love with me. I thought he was and now I'm not sure if I'm in love with him either. I have an awful feeling I just want his money. Otherwise I will have to sell the house.'

'Does everything come down to the house?' Kelvin said and she was even more ashamed.

When Kelvin had had his tea and gone out she asked her parents whether they would come and live with her at the hall.

'Eh, Erin, we couldn't do that,' her mother said.

'But why not? It's lovely.'

'I wouldn't like leaving my neighbours and friends—'

'But when Dad can't work any more then what will you do?'

'Kelvin has said he'll take care of us. He's been like a son to us since he came home. He's a good pitman and he'll have this house and we'll be able to stay here where we belong.'

The child in Erin wanted to stamp her feet and cry and protest that they would rather stay in a little pit row than go to live in the most wonderful house she had ever seen with big rooms and lovely gardens but then her mother said, 'We would never fit into a place like that. We belong in Lilac Street.'

And she knew that it was right, that her parents would be

lonely there. So when she ended up sitting over the fire it seemed to her that Broke Hall was so empty and echoing that she was afraid for the first time and thought longingly of her parents and Kelvin sitting over the front-room fire in Lilac Street and she resented that they did not need her.

Diana had moved out of the house without being asked. Erin had no idea where she had gone and she felt so guilty about it. She had thought she would hate the library, have such bad memories of it that she would not be able to live there, but when she went back the garden, though neglected, was full of spring flowers.

There were blackbirds on the lawns, blossom on the trees in the tiny orchard and when she went into the house the sunlight was falling in coloured sunbeams through the stained glass in the hall and the library was serene, no evidence that anything had ever gone wrong.

She was not sure what she would live on. Allan had offered to lend her money. He did not offer to marry her even though he was about to be divorced and she hardly dared to mention it to him.

The thing for her to do, she felt sure, was to become pregnant, then, if he was the man she thought he was, he would have to marry her, be glad to perhaps though since he already had a son she was not sure of her ground here. However, she was not pregnant and Allan, while enthusiastic enough for her body, was somehow unapproachable and spending a great deal of time at work.

Now that he had so successfully defended her the scandal between them did not seem so important and lots of people wanted him to represent them. She had not minded when she was a part of work but now that she was not he did not seem inclined to spend much time at her house and she had no inclination to leave it except for necessities.

Allan was keeping her and the house and she did not like the idea. It was as though he was paying to go to bed with her because they did not have much time for one another apart from this. What with his work, his divorce and his child, Allan was a very busy man.

Laurie was sometimes at home for brief holidays and

although Allan said he did not see much of his child it was obvious to her that he did and she did not want anything to do with Laurie once she had met him and that by mistake. She had turned up at Allan's house without being asked and was ushered into the drawing room to see a child who as far as she could judge was the complete image of Kaye Jamieson, skinny, fair and silent.

Allan introduced them and the little boy sat as though he were made of stone. Erin knew nothing about children, had no idea what to say, and was very aware of the fact that Allan's child instantly hated her, possibly even before he met her because she was stealing his father.

When she ventured to say so later to Allan he said, 'Oh no, it wasn't you. Laurie doesn't like me,' in such an objective way that she was upset for him. 'It isn't that he minds us, it's just that he loves Kaye and like Kaye doesn't care for the talk. You can hardly blame him for that.'

Allan, she thought, could have been speaking about other people for all the emotion coming off him and she thought it was one of his gravest faults that he was so withdrawn, that he backed away from people, accepted their judgement of him.

Allan spent all his time wanting to see Laurie and then wishing he hadn't. The child was sullen. Who could blame him? Allan was obliged to go to Jake's parents to pick up his son and there he was pointedly ignored, kept in the hall, never even caught a glimpse of Kaye.

The boy would come to him, closing the door of whatever room he had come out of and Allan would see nobody but the maid who answered the front door. After being treated to a half-day silence from his son no matter what he did on two occasions, Allan said to him as he took him back, 'We don't have to do this any more if you don't want to.'

He stopped the car.

Laurie didn't say anything.

'I won't come here again until you ask,' Allan said.

They sat there in silence for a long time and then Laurie opened the car door and bolted.

Twenty-Four

Mr Fortnum, the clerk who had worked with Lilian at Jake's chambers, came to see her. He had been very kind to her. She was surprised to see him.

'I didn't expect you.'

'I know. I know. I hope I'm not intruding, Mrs Coulthard, but we miss you in chambers and I was concerned to see that you and Nora were well and that you like your new job.'

Lilian welcomed the change and she realized then that she didn't just miss Jake, she missed the people she had worked with. She hadn't yet got to know the people at her new office and the work by comparison was dull. Also it paid less and she needed more money.

'The thing is . . .' Mr Fortnum stopped. 'Correct me if I'm wrong but it did seem to the people in Mr Jake's chambers' – Lilian had no idea why his staff called him 'Mr Jake', instead of Mr Armstrong, but she had the feeling that a lot of them had worked for his father and been passed on to Jake because they were reliable and good at their jobs – 'that he took a shine to you.'

Took a shine to, what a lovely expression, Lilian thought, as though something bright was between them when in fact it was the very opposite.

'Mr Fortnum—'

'I know. I know. I'm an interfering old busybody and I should mind my own business—'

'Mr . . . Mr Armstrong has somebody else.'

Mr Fortnum stared at her. 'I don't think he has.'

'I think you'll find . . .' Lilian said and then stopped. She couldn't betray Jake to his staff. And then Mr Fortnum surprised her.

'The lady in question . . . it wouldn't do,' he said.

Lilian stared. 'How did you know?'

'It's the business we're in. We get to know everything about everybody and . . . I saw you when she came to chambers.'

'He doesn't . . . he didn't . . .'

'He cares about you,' Mr Fortnum said. 'Are you going to be proud because he made a mistake?'

'A mistake?'

'Sometimes things are very confusing,' Mr Fortnum said. 'Don't you think it was a mistake?'

'Certainly I did, but . . .'

'Well, then?'

'He . . .' She couldn't tell Mr Fortnum that Jake had slept with Allan Jamieson's wife. That was how she thought of her, as his wife, not by her name, that was too difficult. She couldn't tell him that Jake had fallen below her standards, she who had had to get married, who hadn't loved Norman anywhere near as much as she loved Jake.

'A man who – who makes that kind of mistake could make another.'

'Very true,' Mr Fortnum said. 'He could go on and on making them until he didn't know the difference between right and wrong but some men are lucky and have a very nice wife to go home to. I did. It was the saving of me. Mr Jake doesn't have that.'

'I know he doesn't.'

'But you blame him for taking what he could get.'

'Mr Fortnum!'

'Well, there's no point in beating about the bush, is there? What are you doing here when you could be married to him and having children and living a decent life? You may never get another chance to do this. Why don't you try?'

'I don't trust him.'

'You have to learn to.'

'What if he did such a thing and we – and we were married? I don't think I could stand that.'

'You can't be so afraid of the future that you aren't prepared to take a chance on a man like that.'

182

'His parents . . .' She couldn't prevent her voice from trembling. 'They don't want him to marry me.'

'No, I don't suppose they do. And will that stop him? It didn't stop him the first time, you know. Madeline Atkins was the daughter of a friend of mine. She had no set-off at all but she was like you, you remind me of her so much and I think you remind Mr Jake of her too, and that's why he likes you. She was a warm, good-hearted girl and everybody who knew and cared about her misses her. Why don't you go and see him?'

'I can't.'

Mr Fortnum looked sorrowfully at her for a few seconds and then more sternly and he said, 'I'm going to regret saying this but are you really willing to give him up to that awful woman? She won't do him any good. She thinks she's better than everybody else and she'll spoil everything if you give her the chance. She's married to another man so no good can come of it.'

'He's got somebody else.'

'Yes, well. Men do,' Mr Fortnum said.

'You'll excuse the man and not the woman?'

'I won't excuse anybody. I won't excuse you if you don't go and see him, Mrs Coulthard. Lilian . . . Think about it. Think about the future you might have, could have. Give him another chance.'

When Mr Fortnum had gone Lilian had a good long think about what he had said and then she realized that he was right, that if she didn't go to Jake he would go on making a mess of his life, men were so silly about these things, and she had nothing here.

It was late and dark by the time she walked down past Elvet Bridge where she and Jake had met for the first time and he had saved her from doing something completely stupid.

She walked down Old Elvet, it wasn't very far to Jake's chambers and the light was on as she had somehow known it would be and the door was not locked, and when she opened his door he was sitting there just like he probably did very often, he and Allan and lots of other men who didn't want to go home, sitting behind his desk.

He didn't look up at first, thinking it was one of the staff, and then he stopped writing and that was when he looked up and he went on and on looking at her, as though he was not quite sure whether he could believe what he was seeing.

'Lilian?'

She shifted the child in her arms.

'I just . . .' she said and then couldn't think what on earth had happened to all the words she had rehearsed on the way and then Nora struggled so much that she had to let go of her and the child ran across to Jake. She held out both arms just as she had done when he had come to visit them when they lived in his house and Jake said her name and pulled her up onto his knee and Nora kissed him. It was exactly what Lilian wanted to do.

Jake got up with the child in his arms and without saying anything else they locked up and walked back to Jake's house and when they had put Nora to bed they came back downstairs and she put from her mind all thoughts of Kaye Jamieson. Jake stood before the front-room fire, hesitating. Lilian put up both arms to his neck and kissed his mouth. Jake folded her against him and put his face into her hair.

'Oh, Lilian,' he said, 'I love you so much. Will you marry me?'

Twenty-Five

That early summer one Sunday afternoon Allan and Erin walked around the gardens together at Broke Hall, she knew that was his favourite bit, just as he loved the arboretum at his own house. There came a point where she could not hold back any longer from saying, 'Are we going to get married?'

'Yes, of course.' The way that he said it made her realize he had been thinking about marriage.

'Will it take long, the divorce?'

'I don't suppose so. I take the blame, you and I get our names in the papers, the whole place calls it adultery and Kaye gets – Kaye gets Laurie and a great deal of my money. That's not fair, it isn't mine, I shouldn't say that.'

'Will she get the house?'

'I thought I would offer. You'll want to live here, won't you?'

'Yes.'

When he said nothing and didn't look at her but at the way that the sun was going down splendidly behind the cathedral, it was Sunday and the bells were ringing for evensong, she could hear them, she said, 'Tell me what you're thinking. I never know.'

'I just wondered, considering the scandal, will you want to go on living here?'

'I'm used to people talking about me now. Will it be very difficult for you to work in Durham?'

'I don't know. I suppose it might.'

'But you would want to be here for your son?'

'Not really. He's away at school almost all the time and he'll go to university.'

The garden was somehow full of silence, in spite of the bells.

'Oh, Allan, we could have half a dozen children.'

'Do you think?'

'I do.'

'There is one other thing.'

'Anything.'

'I'd want to bring the servants with me, Mrs Mackenzie and Mary and Joe, and Fiona and Albert. They matter a lot to me, I can't manage without them.'

'I can hardly object to that,' she said. 'It'll be wonderful to have help.'

'Mrs Mackenzie is a little bit keen on me, Kaye never liked her.'

'I shall like her, for your sake.'

'I do love you,' he said and that was what she remembered in the middle of the night, the way that he said it, as though he was trying to convince himself and when she awoke for the second time he was standing at the window and she realized the truth. He was never going to love her as he had loved his blasted wife and Kaye was a complete and utter bitch. Why did men love women like that?

It was the first time in weeks that he had consented to stay the night. He would get over Kaye. But what if he didn't? What if every time they met – and they would in such a small city – he thought about Kaye, looked across rooms at her and remembered how good they had been together and as for his son, the spoiled little brat – and then she stopped and thought how hard it must have been, not seeing Allan for five years except for a day or two and growing up without him.

The truth was that children needed their parents a lot less than parents needed their children and it was a problem that got bigger and bigger. She had no doubt that Allan missed and longed for his child.

She sat up in bed.

'When Laurie comes home for the holidays he can come and stay with us.'

Allan turned from the window and then he came back to her, smiling.

'How did you know I was thinking about him?'

'Will you get over Kaye?'

'I'm already over her,' he said and then he came back to

186

bed and kissed her and held her and she forgot about Kaye and Laurie and all the problems and she thought about Allan and the house and how happy they would be.

Laurie came home for his summer holidays taller, thinner and tanned. He wouldn't see his father, he even said he had met 'that woman', but when there was no further discussion of him seeing Allan she asked him about it and Laurie said, 'I don't care if I never see him again. He doesn't either.'

They were having their evening meal. She had grown to hate her uncle and aunt's house by the river. Even more so since Jake had brought Lilian Coulthard and her wretched child and announced that they were to be married and to Kaye's surprise his parents had seemed relieved. No doubt they were glad that there would be no scandal. Kaye had stood the scene as long as she could, lips stiff and then retreated up to her bedroom.

'Why do you say that?' she asked Laurie now.

'It's what he said to me. When he left me here the last time at Whit he said we don't have to see one another again until I choose.'

'And why do you think he said that?'

Laurie looked guiltily at her.

'I think it was something to do with the way I hadn't spoken to him the whole time. I've got nothing to say to him. I think he's horrible. My friends think he's horrible too and they talk about that – that woman. I don't want to see him again in my whole life.'

Allan was supposed to be moving with the servants to Broke Hall but he put it off day after day. He had so much work to do and he was beginning to enjoy it.

He had thought that considering the scandal the local people wouldn't come to him any more but these were the kind of people whose lives were hard and they needed his help. It was the sort of thing he had done before the war, it didn't necessarily make much money but it was the work his father had done and that he had sworn to carry on. The scandal may have harmed his reputation but the fact that he had won a seemingly impossible case made his office busy as never before.

187

It was only when Erin appeared in the office doorway one Saturday night that he realized he hadn't seen her all week.

'I thought you were coming over,' she said, looking rather cross.

'Sorry. Just busy.'

She came in.

'It's Saturday night, Allan, it's half-past seven and I was expecting you at six.'

'I never finish at six.'

Erin looked at him. 'This is what you did to Kaye, isn't it?'

'Did what?'

'Made your work the excuse not to be anywhere.'

'It isn't an excuse.'

'No, it's your whole life,' she said. 'You don't come to the house—'

'I want my divorce through first.'

'You could visit. The butcher visits more often than you do.'

Allan said nothing.

'You haven't seen your son?'

'No, I haven't seen him.'

'Perhaps you should.'

'I'm not going there until I'm asked.'

'That could be a long wait.'

'Very likely.'

'You know, Allan, if you've changed your mind about this, you just have to say so. I'm not going to try and hold you against Kaye and Laurie and I certainly don't want you to feel obliged to be with me.'

'I know that.'

'Do you? But you don't come to the house. Are you seeing someone else?'

Allan got up.

'Of course I'm not. I've never done such a thing in my life.'

'Haven't you?'

'Kaye left me.'

'Only when she found out we were having an affair.'

Allan didn't answer that. Erin went. He thought about getting up and going after her but somehow he couldn't get off the chair and when there was silence again he worked

188

for another hour and then went home.

Mrs Mackenzie came into the hall when she heard him and smiled and told him the dinner would not be long and she had just poured him a drink so he went into the library and there on a silver tray a Scotch and soda awaited him.

He stood there by the open window and that was when he realized that he couldn't leave. He never wanted to live anywhere but here and he didn't want to marry Erin, she had been right. Even if Kaye never came back he couldn't leave.

The following morning he drove across the town and up to Broke Hall. A surprised looking Erin let him in.

'Has something happened?' she said.

'I can't leave my house and I can't marry you. I'm sorry.'

They went inside. Wind and rain had soaked the garden. When she had closed it out Allan followed her into the sitting room.

'I know you can't keep this house on without my help—'

'I'm not going to,' she said softly and when he looked at her in surprise she threw a straight look back at him and she said, 'I'm not as foolish as I used to be. I'm going to offer the house to Diana. It's morally hers. I'm going back to Lilac Street if my parents will have me. I don't think I ever really loved you, it's just that you're so . . . so very special. I never belonged here. I always wanted to but I don't and if it hadn't been for the war things would have been very different. I know I would have married Kelvin. John would have been here and . . . It's no good wishing. Will you ask Kaye to have you back?'

'No.'

She came to him and kissed him.

'I think you should,' she said.

Erin went to see Diana, to Jesmond in Newcastle. She was surprised to see how beautiful a house it was, an elegant Georgian house in its own grounds and Diana looked not happy because she was unhappy to see Erin but content.

'What do you want?' was all she said, after Erin had been shown into a sitting room which looked out across the tennis courts.

'I'm sorry to just arrive like this.'

'How did you find out where I was staying?'

'Mr Saunders, the solicitor, he found out for me. I don't mean to bother you. I just came to tell you that I'm leaving Broke Hall.'

'Leaving it?' Diana had gone pale.

'It is yours, your family has always lived there.'

'You own it, it's nothing to do with me,' Diana said stiffly.

'Diana, I didn't kill him, I know you think I did but the fact remains that I would never kill anyone.'

'I don't think anything of the kind,' Diana said and then she paused and said, 'Do sit down. Would you like some tea?'

'No, thank you.'

'I sometimes think it would have been easier to let him die but I couldn't do it. We had lost everything by the time you got there. I should never have let the marriage go ahead. There was nothing useful in it for either of you. I just wanted to try and give him a little happiness and to take the burden off myself to a certain extent, I suppose.'

'I know. But you won't come back?'

'No, I won't.' Diana smiled suddenly. 'As a matter of fact I'm getting married. My cousins introduced me to a nice man.'

'I see. I'm very pleased for you. Well then, I shall have to sell the place unless you want it, I can't afford to keep it on.'

Diana's eyes glittered.

'I thought Allan Jamieson was a rich man.'

'I'm going back to Lilac Street. I shall sell the Hall and send you half the money and it will help you to buy a new house for your new life and it will help me to make my parents more comfortable and . . . perhaps more.'

Allan spent a great deal of time wanting to see Laurie but doing nothing about it until one evening that summer when he was still in his chambers and he heard the outer door and said, 'I'm in here. Who is it?' and a small head came round the door and Laurie said,

'It's me. I . . . I came to see you.'

Allan stared at him. He wanted to say stupid things like 'haven't you grown' and 'what on earth are you doing here' but most of all he wanted to ask about Kaye.

'Come in,' was all he said. Laurie came in, closing the door.

'I just wanted to tell you that I'm not going back to London to school. They are trying to make me, Mummy and Uncle Reggie and . . . and the others but Uncle Jake . . . Uncle Jake's all right,' Laurie said and subsided into a chair. 'Are you still seeing that woman?'

Allan was rather stunned at the amount Laurie had to say. He was like a bottle of beer shaken and then opened.

'Lady Ballantine. Sometimes, yes.'

'Why?'

'She likes me. Difficult to think, isn't it?' Allan couldn't help the sarcasm.

'Don't you like Mummy any more at all? You never see her.'

'She doesn't like me.'

'That isn't what I asked you.' He would make a fine barrister, Allan couldn't help thinking.

'Yes, I like both of you,' he said.

'If you do then why can't you ask us to come back and live with you at home? It is our home.'

Allan couldn't think of anything that would make a decent reply.

'Does she live there with you?'

'No.'

'Is she going to be your next wife?'

'No.'

'Then why can't we come back?'

'You can if you want.'

'You would have to ask Mummy.'

'All right.'

'You will try to say the right things to her?'

'I'll try.'

'Promise?'

'I promise.'

'You won't go away?'

'What makes you think I'm going anywhere?'

'Mummy says you might. I don't you to go away. I don't want to be left here without you. Promise me you won't go.'

'I won't go anywhere without telling you.'

191

Laurie seemed satisfied with that. Allan suggested he should take him home and he nodded.

They didn't speak on the way back to South Street but instead of leaving him there and driving off Allan got out of the car with him and went into the house. Henry was standing in the hall and obviously didn't know what to say.

'I'd like to speak to Kaye,' Allan said.

'Yes, of course. Do come in. Laurie—'

But Laurie had already run along the hall and disappeared into the depths of the house. Henry ushered Allan into a small sitting room and after hesitating for a second he went out. Five minutes went past, seven and just when Allan was beginning to think this had been a mistake his wife came into the room. She was wearing a very pretty dress, cream with tiny pink flowers, as though she might be going somewhere.

'Going out?' he ventured.

'As a matter of fact we've been to a matinee. I didn't realize he'd left the house until about half an hour ago. I didn't know Laurie had gone to you. Thank you for bringing him back.'

'I wish you'd told me there was a problem about school.'

'And have you blame yourself, as you blame yourself for everything else?'

'I blame you for some of it.'

Kaye's blue eyes sparkled.

'Do you indeed?' she said.

'Is Laurie going to go to school here?'

'That is the general idea,' she said. 'You should be pleased. Your son is as stubborn as you are.'

Allan made himself say the next bit because he had promised himself that he would but he would have given a great deal not to.

'I want you to come back.'

The sparkle went. She stared at him. She didn't say anything.

'Are you going to tell me you're happy here?' he said when he decided that he had waited for long enough.

'I wasn't happy with you.'

'So you want to divorce me?'

'I'm assured it's the best thing to do.'

'Are you? He isn't much of a lawyer, then, is he? Did he

tell you that if we divorced I would make sure you received as little money as possible?'

'Yes.'

'Did he tell you that you won't get the house?'

'Yes.'

'Did he tell you that I might fight you for Laurie?'

'He didn't tell me that you would make threats.'

'The law was made by men for men. Don't you realize that, Kaye?'

'Yes, I realize it.'

'But you still want rid of me? Very well, then. I never intended to fight over Laurie, you may have the house if you choose—'

'I don't want your blessed house,' Kaye said loudly, 'and don't tell me what I can have and what I can't. You're too keen on telling people what to do. I'm your wife. Don't damned well tell me what to do.'

'And there is a great deal of money—'

'I don't want your money either. You always assumed I married you for who you were and how much you had and it isn't true. I married you because I couldn't help it, because I adored you, and what did you do?'

'Yes, what did I do?'

'You held everything against me, like you always do with people. Nobody holds a grudge as well as you. You were so busy winning the bloody war single-handedly that you didn't give me your time, your regard or your respect and then you . . . and then you went and had an affair with that dreadful girl.'

'She's not a dreadful girl,' was all Allan managed. 'Besides,' he added, after a moment or two, 'you had Jake.'

'Oh, Jake,' she said, as though he didn't matter. 'He's going to marry Lilian Coulthard.'

'So he should. Are you going to come home?'

'No.'

'I do love you, Kaye. I've always loved you.'

Kaye tossed her head.

'Why do men think those few words will do it?'

'A last resort, perhaps? So you won't?'

'No,' Kaye said and she flounced out of the room.

Allan knew that he should have left but he stood by the fire during the five minutes that followed and tried to compose himself and then the door opened and he turned hopefully. It was Laurie.

'Mummy does nothing but cry,' he said, 'and it's horrid living here with Uncle Henry and Auntie Maude. They don't like you and they talk about you all the time. Auntie Maude says that Uncle Jake should have won the case. Uncle Jake's not as clever as you.'

'It wasn't actually anything to do with that,' Allan said.

'What was it to do with, then?'

'Luck, like most things. I ought to go.'

'I'd like to come and stay with you at the house.'

'How about next week?'

Allan left, waving to Laurie as he went. It was only when he had manoeuvred the car onto the main road and out towards his own house that he admitted to himself that he did not want to go home. He wanted to be where Kaye was. He wanted her in Hedleyhope House and Laurie safe in bed and for the evening to come down and protect and hold them and for there to be night after night for them to spend by the fire together until they became old and had memories.

Erin stood the loneliness for several more weeks but she found that she was spending more and more time in Lilac Street and each time she went there she was the more reluctant to go back to Broke Hall. She found a buyer for it and convinced herself that if her parents did not want her she could afford to buy or rent a small house in Durham even after giving Diana her half of the money from the sale.

Her mother was always offering to make meals for her and by the end of the summer had taken to saying as she was leaving, 'Why don't you stay the night, your room's there and ready for you,' and she wished more and more that she could say yes.

Her parents were surprised that she was selling Broke Hall but they knew that she had no money and when she told them that she and Allan were not to be married she could see by their faces how relieved they were but they did not interfere, they did not speak the magic words which she wished to hear.

Broke Hall got bigger and bigger and less and less like anywhere that she wanted to be. She could not wait to get rid of the house that she had thought she loved so much. She could not put from her mind how unhappy she and Angus had been there. It was another life, it was over and all she wanted was to get out. She was even grateful to Allan that he had effectively stopped her from being able to afford to live there.

When they met at the house for the last time she was amazed that she had even thought she was in love with him. He was not a good-looking young man, he looked tired, thin, edgy, not at all like Kelvin, who was full of energy. Every time she went back to Heath Houses he suggested going for walks, having outings, and he talked non-stop to her and made her laugh and the more time she spent with him the more she wanted to be there.

He shyly asked if she would have tea in town with him one afternoon that September and it was one of those lovely days when the leaves were beginning to change colour and some of them littered the towpath. They went for a walk up to Prebends Bridge and all along the river before coming back to a teashop and they demolished cream cakes and several cups of tea and when Erin thought afterwards about her feelings she knew that they had all been positive. She hated going back to Broke Hall, she hated being alone.

As they walked back through the town and over Framwellgate Bridge they stopped and leaned over the bridge and looked at the way that half the leaves had come off the trees and made the view of the castle and cathedral so much clearer and she said to Kelvin, 'When the money comes through from the house I thought maybe you might like to help me find somewhere to live.'

He hesitated, studying the view.

'I could do,' he said.

'Don't you want to?'

'No, not much.'

'Why not?'

Kelvin glanced at her and then he said, 'Because I wish you would come back and live in Lilac Street.'

Her heart beat hard.

'I can't. Not unless my mam and dad ask me.'

'They don't like to ask you.'

'I don't blame them for that.'

'And I can't.'

'Can't you? Why not?'

'Because you'll have money and . . . I haven't got any.'

She considered.

'So I have to live on my own because I can afford to. That doesn't make sense.'

'It's not my house,' he said. 'Your parents were kind enough to make a home for me when I had nobody else to go to. I wouldn't presume to tell them what to do. I care about them too much for that. Your mother's . . . well, she's like a mother to me too and your dad's just . . . he's just grand.'

'You said in court . . . you said you loved me.'

'I did.'

'Does that mean you don't now?'

Kelvin didn't answer and the view from the bridge had obviously become fascinating to him.

'If you don't I'll go and buy a house in the town and not bother you any more. Have you found another lass?' she said.

'Of course I haven't,' he said flatly. 'Look, I have to go,' and he went off and left her standing there.

She watched him all the way until he turned up Framwellgate and was lost to sight.

When she got back to Broke Hall she couldn't settle and would have given anything to have been able to go home but she didn't feel as if she could go. She didn't feel as if she would ever be able to.

It was mid-evening by the time the darkness came down and just as she was closing the curtains in the sitting room she thought she caught sight of some movement in the garden and when she looked harder she could see three figures wending their way up from the river through the gardens towards the hall, two men, one rather short and the other much taller, both in caps, and a woman, an older woman, wearing a very nice hat, a hat which she instantly recog-

196

nized, it was her mother's best going-to-church and special-occasions hat.

With a glad cry she ran through the hall and opened the front door.

'Well,' her mother said as they reached the top of the hill and she could stop for breath, 'you didn't seem to be coming home so we thought we'd better come and see you. Get the kettle on, our Erin, I'm parched.'

They came in, admiring the house as they did so but when they were seated around the fire drinking tea her father said, just as shy as Kelvin had been that afternoon, 'We understand from young Kelvin here that you might be inclined to come home to live. We don't want to push you but we would like you to if you still want.'

'Oh yes, I do,' Erin said steadily.

'Well, then,' her mother said, 'that's settled. I could manage another cup of tea if I was asked.'

Laurie turned up at Hedleyhope House one evening shortly after this. Allan thought he should have been surprised but he wasn't and was so pleased to see his son that he had to stop himself from hugging Laurie, who would have been mortified. He didn't like to point out that Laurie should have been at school that day because Laurie chatted freely about the things he had done, played billiards, taken the dogs out.

'Does your mother know you're here?'

Laurie assured him so blithely that she did that Allan was again not very surprised when an hour later Kaye turned up in Henry's Daimler, sweeping into the driveway in a slight skid which did nothing to make Allan think she was in a good temper. Laurie looked dismayed, said, 'Oh hell,' and disappeared.

Allan walked down the front steps as Kaye got out of the car.

'He's here,' Allan said.

She was relieved, he could see, and then angry.

'Where?' was all she said and a lanky figure ran into the back of Allan and clutched at him and said loudly, 'I'm not coming back. I'm staying here with Daddy.'

'No, you're not,' Allan said, dragging him around to face his mother.

197

'I'll run away.'

'You're very naughty,' Kaye said.

'At least I'm not bad and wicked like you two,' Laurie said hanging on to the front of Allan's jacket.

'Why don't you come inside?' Allan said to them both and took Laurie's arm and they went into the drawing room.

It was, Allan thought with admiration, the most beautiful room in a house filled with exquisite rooms. It was a kind of very pale blue with white surroundings, two huge fireplaces and great big windows which looked all the way down the valley to the arboretum, the trees nothing but dark shadows now in the evening.

The fires were wood and both were lit and the lamps cast soft glows over the thick Turkish rugs spread across an oak floor. There were little areas of chairs and sofas grouped because it was such a big room and it was homely too, there were books and magazines on tables and one of those revolving bookcases which he liked so much.

He was rather satisfied with how Kaye looked at it. The house in South Street was pretty but they had nothing like this and very small gardens because there was so little room.

'It looks lovely,' she said.

'Would you like some tea?'

'I would like a drink if it's all the same to you.'

Allan poured her whisky and soda and soda for Laurie and she refused a seat and stood by the nearer of the two fires, saying nothing.

'I could bring Laurie back in the morning.'

'That would be very kind,' she said.

'Can we play a board game?' Laurie suggested eagerly.

Allan thought it was a foolish suggestion but it turned out to be much better than that because they sat around the fire, at a little table, and nobody had to talk and Laurie won when he was excited and the evening went on almost easily until Laurie fell asleep in his big chair and then the game ceased. The clock was striking eleven.

'I ought to go.'

'Why not leave your car and I'll take you?'

'I'm perfectly capable of driving myself. You will bring him back in the morning?'

'Why don't you let him spend some time here, just a few days?'

'Because he would refuse to come back. He wants to be here.'

'Don't you want to be here?'

She was almost at the car but she turned and looked at him in the windy moonlight and she said, 'Yes, I do.'

'Kaye, you can have the house. I'll move out.'

Kaye didn't answer for a moment and then she said, 'It isn't the house which is important to Laurie, it's you. Do you think he wouldn't follow you to Broke Hall or wherever you go?'

'Broke Hall is sold and I'm not going anywhere.'

'She sold it?'

'Erin has gone back to live with her parents in Heath Houses.'

'Then you're not seeing her?'

'You thought I was, when I'd asked you to come back here?'

'I didn't know,' Kaye said stiffly. 'I thought it was Laurie you were concerned about, not me and that you would do anything for him. I know I would.'

'Then why don't you stay here just for a day or two? We'll sort something out.' When she hesitated he said, 'You still have clothes here and your own room, I'm not going to bother you.'

'I told my aunt I'd be back, with Laurie.'

'She'll understand, surely?'

'She'll think something's happened to me. I must go.'

'I could send a message. I'm sure Albert wouldn't mind going.'

'I have Henry's car.'

'He can walk to chambers. It'll do him good. Please stay, just for a little while.'

Still Kaye hesitated.

'Very well, then,' she said finally.

When they went back inside Laurie awoke and Kaye took him upstairs to bed while he asked questions which she fended off as they climbed the stairs. Allan didn't dare to expect that she would come back downstairs but she did.

'Are you going to chambers tomorrow?'

'I don't have to. It's Saturday.'

'You have a lot of work now?'

'Yes.'

'The kind of work you used to like, helping poor people. It doesn't make any money.'

'That's exactly the kind,' Allan said with a slight smile.

'I'm glad you are. It used to make you happy, I'm sure it could again.'

Mrs Mackenzie appeared without being summoned.

'I'm going off to bed now, unless there's anything else. I have left a light supper in the dining room.'

Mrs Mackenzie, Allan couldn't help thinking, fancied herself as a matchmaker. The candles were lit in the dining room. Wine had been opened and there was the appetizing smell of roast chicken and warm bread.

'And I thought she didn't like me,' Kaye said, ruefully.

'I think she could be resigned to you.'

'Oh, thank you.'

'So could I.'

'That's extremely kind of you, Allan.'

'I would hate to overwhelm you with flattery and compliments.'

Kaye smiled.

'I shall have to go back first thing in the morning,' she said as she sat down.

Allan thought he wasn't hungry but he had had nothing to eat since breakfast and once he began to tuck into rather big chicken sandwiches it was difficult not to eat too fast. Kaye looked about her.

'I had almost forgotten how beautiful your house is.'

'It's our house.' Kaye didn't say anything. 'Doesn't it feel like yours at all? Even when Laurie's asleep upstairs?'

'He's an extremely devious child.'

'I would like him to have both parents.'

'You mean two more than you had?'

'Something like that, yes.'

'He would still have two if we were divorced.'

'I don't want to get divorced,' Allan said and then couldn't eat the rest of his sandwich and put it down on his plate and looked at it.

Kaye didn't say anything and she wasn't eating. Then she said, 'Neither do I but I suspect for different reasons.'

'And what are those?'

'Divorced women are looked down on, shunned by society and . . . forgive me, Allan, you're a rich man and rich men are always acceptable. I don't want to spend the rest of my life alone.'

'I doubt that would happen. Please stay here, even if it's just because you don't want to be alone.'

'Just for tonight.'

'All right, then.'

It was strange for Kaye going into the bedroom which had been hers for so long. It hadn't been touched except to be cleaned, all the things which had been hers which she had left were still exactly as they had been. The wardrobes were full of her clothes, the bathroom held the soaps which she preferred. It was as if she had been there all the time. She wandered the room for a while and then watched the night progress through the garden. She finally undressed but she didn't get into bed, she went softly into Allan's room and it was as she had suspected, he was not even undressed but stood by the fire.

'I knew you hadn't gone to bed. Are you brooding?' she said.

He looked at her and smiled.

'Hoping,' he said.

'Hoping what?'

'Hoping that I might be able to ask you to stay another day when the morning comes and that you might say yes.' He spoke lightly.

'You've changed,' Kaye said.

'Is that for the better?'

'I haven't decided yet. You're starting to enjoy the work again, I think, and that Laurie hasn't gone away to school. He must go to school eventually, you know. They have said they'll have him at the school here and it's a nice place and they have a very good view of the cathedral from the school chapel.'

201

'Oh well, we must send him there, then,' Allan said. 'If the view's good.'

'Where else?'

'I didn't mean it.' She was close enough for him to take her very carefully into his arms. 'I'm just so glad you're here.'

'I must go back in the morning.'

'You said.'

'I did, didn't I? I'm so afraid.'

'There's nothing to be afraid of.'

'I don't think people can go back.'

'We won't go back, we'll go on.'

'I'd like to, but . . . Allan, I didn't mean what I said about why I didn't want a divorce. I don't think I can bear the rest of my life without you.'

Allan kissed her. She hesitated and then kissed him too.

Outside in the hall Laurie waited for a moment or two and then ran back into his own bed and jumped into the middle of it. It was much better here than at Uncle Henry's. His Uncle Reg smelled disgustingly of drink, Jake had gone and his Uncle Henry and Auntie Maude were just so old. Best of all it didn't look like he would ever have to go back to that awful school with the grey corridors and grey class-rooms and grey dormitories.

He got into bed and snuggled down and tried to think how much longer they would allow him not to go to school at all. He hoped it would be a good long time, a very good long time, maybe even up to Christmas, and then he lay in the darkness and tried to think what he would like best for Christmas. He thought he would probably get lots of presents and maybe it would snow.

He would like a big wooden sledge, a toboggan, red so that when it did snow he would be able to sledge all the way down to the river, past the trees which his dad liked so much, past the heathers, the big white birch trees, the bamboos and then the waterfalls which tumbled at last into the stream at the bottom of the hill. He would never again leave his parents, he would stay here and keep an eye on them and come home from school every night. It would be the best Christmas ever, he decided. The very best.

202